ALENA CERULEAN

Sorceress in the City

A Lesbian, Mind Control Erotica

Contents

Chapter 1: Dark and Stormy

My mothers warned me it wouldn't be easy to make a living off my magic.

Perfecting my skills meant neglecting more practical talents like balancing my checking account or riding a bicycle. The ability to commune with the dead, levitate a car, and compel someone to tell the truth sounds amazing (and it is), but finding a way to make money using magic...

Yeah, that's the real trick.

That's what led me to my favorite bar downtown. The sign on the outside of the place identifies this as The Lake, but that's just for the normal people. For them, this place is a small dive bar no bigger than my living room. The drink selection fits on a coaster, and the service comes with a free side of surliness.

There's a connecting room just past the bathrooms that looks like a small library. The room is so tiny that its three walls are each made up of a narrow bookshelf. A bouncer stands by the door and if you don't know the password, you don't get in.

Tonight's bouncer is a woman with arms so muscular they

could break my head open like a nutcracker. Her hair runs down her back in a long, pink braid. I once had my short, brown hair dyed that color, but I can't afford the indulgence these days.

"Private party." She doesn't bother raising a hand to stop me, because she recognizes me.

"I left my sword at home." I don't own a sword, but that's the password for the week.

The bouncer steps aside and let's me enter. I push on the bookshelf on the far wall. It slides open and admits me to the bar within the bar: Avalon.

The subdued glow of candlelight and a woman's voice singing "The Nearness of You" greets me.

There aren't many places in this city where the magical and mythical among us can gather and be open about ourselves, but Avalon is one of them. The ceiling and floor are painted black and the walls are covered in mirrors, giving the impression the room goes into infinity.

The bar made of dark wood is just inside the door and has three sides to it. Most of the stools around it are occupied even though it's a Tuesday night. The only man here is the one behind the bar. Men don't get in unless a woman vouches for him, but if he doesn't behave himself, both get banned.

"Hey, Monica!" The guy on the sober side of the bar waves me over to him near the service flap. Hector is bald and easy on the eyes, if you like his type, which most of Avalon's patrons don't, myself included. The owner saves Tanith and Selene for the busier nights.

I lean against the wall by the service flap and cross my arms as I glance over the patrons. I don't see the person I'm meeting at the bar or any of the booths along the wall. I offer a smile to

Hector as I look back to him. "I'm meeting a potential client tonight. She said she'd be wearing a purple jacket."

Hector answers with a "no shit" scowl. I'm not used to that kind of reception from him.

"I had to move her to a private booth in the back room. Every fucking fairy, banshee, vampire, and dragon in this place was hitting on her. Thought they were gonna run her off. Hell, a few of them acted like they were winding up to fight over her."

"Seriously?" I can't help but think he's exaggerating, because Avalon isn't that kind of place.

"Yeah, so do me a favor," he says as he grabs a bottle of ginger beer to make my usual, "keep her ass back there until you're done and then get her out of here."

While I'm waiting for Hector to finish my dark and stormy, I look over the crowd. He's summed up most of the patrons for the night. They seem in good spirits for a group that had a few ready to throw hands not that long before I got here. I take in a deep breath that includes the collective smoke of candles, cigars, and cigarettes. You can't reasonably follow city ordinances for smoking in a bar frequented by dragons, even when they're in their more human form.

I steady my thoughts and think the incantation to heighten my soul's sight. The spell doesn't require carefully pronounced words or precisely drawn runes. Most don't. A proper incantation is composed of a thought, and teaching it to another is like explaining the color vermilion to someone who's been blind all their lives. Sure, you can do it, but it's pretty damn hard. It's the difference between saying the formula "E equals MC squared" and actually understanding what the Theory of Relativity means without needing to apply words or numbers to it.

Closing my eyes, I study the people in this room. I see them all as auras, and the color of their light pulses with a rhythm that shares their feelings and all the things that make them who and what they are. I don't notice it at first, but the longer I look at them with my soul, I realize how aroused they all are. When I open my eyes and rely on my normal sight, I notice how many are huddled close. Some in the booths are playfully touching one another. Some are just holding hands, but others are kissing. My eyes linger on a couple making out in one of the booths, because one of them resembles one of my many exes with long blonde hair that flows in waves. She's even dressed similar to how Evan used to in a green, velvet top with a generous v neck that I can't help but stare at as my heart beats a little faster.

Hector knocks loudly on the bar top in front of me. "Earth to Monica!" He points to the highball glass with my drink.

"Thanks." I pick it up and take a long sip. The burn of the ginger beer outweighs the rum and lime, helping me focus on why I'm here.

I make my way through the crowd, doing my best to avoid looking at "not-Evan."

The doors to the back room are frosted glass. The room is darker than usual since it's not hosting an event tonight. The only light comes from the candle on the table in the corner booth. The way the tall wall of the booth is shaped, it hides most of the view.

Only once I'm right up to the booth do I see my prospective client. Now I understand the fuss, because I stop in my tracks and can't find my voice. She has straight auburn hair with tanned skin. Her black strapless top is paired with a silver paisley, partial corset. Her purple jacket is folded up and resting on the seat next to her. The light of the candle sparkles in her

4

cerulean eyes which fix on me.

"Are you Monica Devlin?" Her voice, smooth as fine scotch, holds a soft burn to it, and I realize she's probably worried I'm yet another patron coming to harass her.

I clear my throat and nod. "You must be Ms. Tennison."

"Please, call me Ceri."

Her full, dark red lips smile up at me, and I'm embarrassed at the small thrill I get from her being glad to see me. I wish I'd dressed up more. Given we're meeting in a bar, I opted to wear a burgundy, button-down shirt beneath a black, military style jacket I got at a renn faire back when I was in college.

"May I join you?"

At her assent, I slide into the booth. The seat, like the small table, is shaped like a circle, although the narrow opening makes more similar to a large capital C. I can't help but wonder why Hector chose this table, because there's very little space between us. Odds favor it was to hide her from anyone's view if they happened to open the door to this room.

As I shift into my spot, I catch the scent of roses on her. Our knees brush against one another which is how I know she's wearing a skirt. The sensation of her legs against mine makes me flush. I steady my breathing as I fight down the growing urge to let my knees brush up against her even more. It's a good thing I wore pants, because if our bare legs were touching one another, I'd be undone.

This isn't like me. Yes, Ceri is gorgeous, but I've been close with many beautiful women in the past without getting this worked up. My suspicion of her centers my mind on why I'm here, because this meeting might not be what it seems. A skilled sorceress is hard to come by. Some see me as a resource to control and take advantage of. I've learned not to be too trusting, which is why I'm meeting Ceri here and not in my home or an office, not that I have an office. This isn't neutral territory, though. While I don't own Avalon, I frequent it enough to consider it my place. What concerns me is that this back room is private. I usually rely on the public setting of the main room to provide a certain level of protection.

"Would you prefer a different table?" I ask, unsure what I want her answer to be. Her legs are tangled with mine. That won't be a problem in the other booths. If we stay here, we could get so much more entwined, and I need to not think about that if I'm going to make certain whether I can trust her.

"I'd rather just get to why I'm here." She brushes her hair back over her shoulder, drawing my eyes to her chest.

"Good. Let's start with how this will work, and please understand that none of this is negotiable." I try as hard as I can to make that a stern declaration, but my attraction to her is distracting. That I'm dropping into a script I've used dozens of times over the years helps me meet her gaze long enough to say what I need to without marveling at the blue of her eyes. "My line of work doesn't come without risks, so I need an assurance that your request is legitimate and without ulterior motives."

I reach into my inside breast pocket and pull out a small vial the size of my pinkie finger with a metal topper screwed on tight. "This is a truth potion. You'll want to mix it with your drink." I tap the base of her wine glass. "The effects will only last about twenty to thirty minutes, but if we finish early, you don't need to worry about anyone else taking advantage of it. The potion only compels you to be truthful to the sorceress who brewed it, which is me."

Potions are one of the trickier things about magic. Much

like the art of incantation, potions aren't set recipes that just anyone can brew, so if you're hoping to search YouTube for a how-to video on love potions, you're out of luck. Brewing them often demands a similar focus of thought as with incantations throughout the process, so the longer a potion takes to create, the harder it is. Truth potions offer an uncomfortable challenge, because they also require the sorceress to confess aloud as many truths as possible to herself. One little white lie or half-truth can ruin the batch. Sorry, Obi-Wan, but none of that "from a certain point of view" stuff works with this. I can already feel a corner of my mind filing away a confession for the next batch: in this moment, I've never wanted to lick another woman's cunt this badly. I have to get control of my thoughts. I'd be tempted to invoke my soul sight again to better study who I'm dealing with, but I don't think I can muster the self-control to perform the incantation.

Ceri picks up the vial and studies it. In the candlelight, the potion looks more green than blue. "Why twenty to thirty minutes?" She wobbles her head side to side as if to shake into place the words she wants to use. "What I mean is why does it vary?"

I lift my dark and stormy for a sip but end up taking a large swallow instead. Goddess bless Hector, because he knows to go light on the rum when I'm here for business. He makes up for the alcohol when I visit Avalon for fun.

"A variety of things can mitigate how long the potion works." I soften my expression, because she looks nervous. Even if the many warnings of my instincts are wrong and her intentions lack any malice to me or another, I can understand why someone wouldn't want to open themselves up this much. I've had more than one prospective client walk away at this point.

Like many women, my mothers warned me before I was even a teenager not to accept a random drink from a stranger. "Body weight is one factor." She doesn't look more than 125 pounds, so that pushes her towards the thirty minutes. "Another is strength of will." Which isn't something even a sorceress can eyeball.

She chuckles nervously as she turns the vial gripped between her fingertips. "Then how will you know when it's stopped working?"

No one I've met has asked that before, and I bite my lower lip as I consider how to best answer that. "I imbued the potion with a small part of my spirit when I brewed it, so I can feel when it's working and when it's not. The part of my soul within the potion returns to me. Once all of it has passed back to me, I know the spell is ended."

Her eyes narrow. "So was this all you brewed?"

"No, I usually make a large batch. It's easier for me that way."

"So this only has a sliver of your spirit in it." She leans back in her seat, and much to my disappointment, I notice her legs pull away from mine as much as the small booth will allow. "So it's not like your soul is whole again when this is done, right?"

I shake my head. "I'm afraid you'll just have to take my word on that part, and I understand if this is something you're unwilling to do."

"But if I don't drink this, you won't take the job."

"Even if you do drink it, I might not." I offer her my most reassuring smile, forgetting for a moment that I need to be suspicious of her. "The point is that I need to know your true intentions. If what you're asking of me might have an ulterior motive to harm me or another, then my answer is almost certainly going to be no."

Chapter 1: Dark and Stormy

She slumps forward a little with a distant look in her eyes as she fidgets with the vial and considers what I've told her. Then she straightens up and untwists the top. "I do hope this isn't going to ruin my Cabernet." She pours the potion into her glass of red wine.

"Mixed into your wine, you'll hardly notice it."

She raises her glass and holds it there until I raise mine, as well. "Here's to the truth," she says.

I take a healthy drink of my dark and stormy. Ceri finishes her wine in one gulp and puts down the empty glass.

With a sheepish grin, she looks left to right. "So," she says the word, dragging it out, "how will I know when it's—" Her eyes widen and she places a hand to her chest. "Oh."

I can feel the potion has already taken hold, too. Typically, it's just a faint whisper of wind through my mind, but this time, it tingles across my skin, starting along my scalp, fingertips, and toes. The sensation makes me laugh a little.

"Well then, let's get started," I say. "Say your name."

She stares at me wide-eyed as if seeing me for the first time. The fascination within her gaze sends a delightful shiver through me, and as her breathing deepens, I'm drawn to the swell of her breasts.

"Cerina Alethea Tennison." She reaches towards me and then stops herself. She stares down at her hand as if it's become a separate being with its own will to guide it. "Should this? I mean, you didn't mention it would feel like this?"

I catch my own breath, forcing myself to speak. "Are you all right? How do you feel?"

She laughs and then licks her lips. "I feel," she says, then pauses less with what seems uncertainty and more like fear, "so aroused. I'm wet, so very wet." She brings her hand to her lips as if to stop the words that have already escaped.

"That." I stop as the tingling sensation that started on the outer portions of my body flows into my breasts and pussy. "I don't know. This doesn't—this hasn't happened with anyone else before."

Her head tilts as she studies me. "You, too? Does this mean you have to speak the truth, too?"

"I don't think so." My answer comes out more certain that I feel. I swallow hard, as if that will somehow stop the mounting urge within me to grab her and pull down her top to suck on her tits. Why is this happening? "Tell me what you want to hire me to do. Quickly!"

"My mother was murdered, and I want to know who did it." She reaches over and takes my hand into hers. She moans, and I muffle a cry of unexpected pleasure that runs from where her fingers touch mine, shooting all the way into my nipples. Ceri forces out the rest of her answer. "She owned a collection of magical artifacts, and whoever killed her stole them. I need them back."

"Ceri, something is wrong." My legs rub together in a growing desperation. I need to cum, and I want her to do it with me.

"It doesn't feel wrong." Her face is slack and almost vacant with lust. Her upper body heaves with growing desire. Her grip on my hand tightens, her fingers entwining with mine. "It feels good." In a gasping voice she whispers, "So good."

My head spins as if I'd downed three shots of tequila. "I need—We've got to—I—Oh, fuck!"

"I want that." She growls as she closes the space between us.

I moan into her kiss. My entire body is electrified with desire, and my nipples are so hard they ache. That makes it all the better when Ceri reaches into my jacket to grab my breast.

Chapter 1: Dark and Stormy

I break from the kiss and lick a bead of sweat from her throat. "Are you doing this?" Even if she is, I'm not sure I'd be able to stop myself if she admitted to it.

"I don't know what's happening." She mewls as I lean in to kiss the swell of her breasts. "Don't stop. Please." Her words devolve into repeated gasps of those three words, and I surrender to them and my own well of overflowing desire.

I should fight this. I need to, but I can't bring myself to stop. My hand finds its way up her skirt, and she cries out as my fingers find that warm, wet place between her legs. She humps against my hand as if doing so hard enough will split apart her panties to let me inside her.

"I need to know more," I say and then nibble at her ear. "What—what do you want me to do when if I find her killer? To kill them?" The notion of killing for her sends an unexpected thrill through me, startling me into a split second of sense. That's a deal-breaker for me. I don't do that, not for anyone. Then she pushes open my shirt, which I didn't realize she'd unbuttoned and shifts my sports bra up to pinch my nipple. I shriek, and any chance I had to regain my self-control evaporates.

"No, not to kill," she says. "I'd want that, but no." I can feel her moan in her throat as I kiss my way down it again. "Need to get back—ohhhh—get back what was taken."

Neither of us speaks then. Her breathing quickens, coming out in sync with her thrusts against my hand. My fingers slip into her soaked panties and stroke her warm folds. No matter how much I know we mustn't do this, I'm too desperate to stop, overcome by whatever this is. A spell out of control? I don't know. The atmosphere of rampant lust in the other room flits through my mind. Tied to this? I can't stop. I stroke her and slip my fingers inside as my other hand rips down the left side of her top. My lips wrap around her nipple, and the taste of her flesh and sweat intoxicate me. She arches her body to push her breast into my eager kiss. Then she throws back her head and her whole body convulses within my grip as she groans long and hard. She languidly squirms against my body until she pushes me away.

A second of panic grips me as she shoves me back against the seat, thinking she's furious with me for what I've just done. Then I see her smile, something befitting a hungry tigress, and I'm transfixed. If I didn't want her before, then I'd drop to my knees for her now.

Ceri leans in towards me and runs a finger across my lips. I kiss and lick her fingers.

"Your turn," she whispers.

Then her other hand slips down into my pants and my drenched panties. I whine as her fingertips find my pussy lips. Now, I'm the one humping like a needy slut, eager to get her touch in me.

"Anything else," she pauses to lick her lips, "you need to ask me?"

I hate my rational mind's efforts to form a question. Yes, there's more I need to know, but most of my brain is so focused on reaching my orgasm that navigating any of my thoughts towards a coherent question delays my true desire. I whine as I manage to speak. "What was stolen that's so important?"

"I don't know what all was taken, but she said some of her artifacts were dangerous."

She slips two fingers into my mouth, and I suck on them. Then her other hand's fingers slip into my pussy. My breath catches as my eyes roll back. Even if she wasn't fucking my mouth with her hand, I couldn't ask a thing. I suck on her fingers as I buck with desperation against her other hand. The way she touches me, it's as if she knows my body's needs and wants better than I do. My entire universe collapses into this need to cum, and the only word I'm capable of thinking is *"Please!"* Then even the ability to form that one word in my mind disappears in a white, blinding burst of blankness as her deft fingers push deep inside me.

When the fog clears in my head, I'm limp against the back cushion of the booth with Ceri nuzzling against me. We both speak in soft, guttural moans as we savor the sensation of our sweaty bodies against one another.

The first words I manage are a hushed "I'm sorry."

She laughs, and in spite of myself, I laugh with her. "Sorry for what?" she asks.

"The potion should not have caused that to happen."

She sits up, and I hold in a groan of complaint as she peels her body off of mine. "I wanted to do that from the moment I saw you."

The potion is wearing off, but it's still got enough of a hold on her for me to know she's not lying. It's possible our mutual attraction and the connection created by the bit of my soul in the potion created some kind of feedback loop of desire, but I've never heard of that happening. Somehow, my theory doesn't feel quite right.

"Still, that shouldn't have happened."

She reaches for her wine glass and then deflates as she realizes the glass is empty. I push my dark and stormy towards her.

"Oh!" She jolts in her seat after she takes a sip, probably not having expected the drink to have that much of a spicy kick to it. "That's very good."

"Dark and stormies are my favorite."

We exchange glances as I take back my glass for a sip. The silence that follows is uncomfortable, but I'm not eager to break it, given what I need to say.

"I feel a little rude talking business after being so intimate, but do know that I will take your case." I pause for another sip of my drink. "And not just because we, uh—you know."

Resting her elbow on the table, Ceri cradles her chin in her hand. "Yes, I assumed as much. I wish I knew what was taken from my mother's home, but I don't. She made me promise to guard those relics with my own life, if something ever happened to her. I've no idea where to begin to find them."

We discuss my rates. I don't share that I'm lowering them for her out of guilt for having lost control as I did. Despite my promise to Hector to get her out of the bar once we're done, I let her walk out without me.

I need a moment to collect myself. Pulling out my cell phone, the time on its display is a little before nine. That's not too late to text either of my mothers. They're both of them skilled in the art of magic, but I'm not sure I care to discuss what happened with them. "Hey, Moms, have either of you ended up so turned on by a truth potion that you and the other person fucked each other senseless?" Yeah, no. I'll pass on that conversation.

Strolling back to the bar, I take one of the open seats and plant my empty glass in front of me. Hector takes it and the look on his face asks without a word if I want another.

I motion with my hand for him to give it to me.

"So how'd the meeting go?" he asks as he drops some ice into a fresh glass.

I snort, and I can't bring myself to meet him in the eye as I answer. "Fine." Oh so very, very fine.

Chapter 1: Dark and Stormy

When he places my second dark and stormy of the night in front of me, I take a sip and then look around the bar. The patrons still seem to be riding the same aroused high as they did before my meeting with Ceri. Is something else going on here? Just in Avalon, or is it wider than that? What happened with Ceri might just be a coincidence and nothing I did with the truth potion. Either way, I make a mental note to be more careful with my client the next time we talk.

For now, I have a drink to finish, and then I've got a case to solve.

Chapter 2: Echoes

The next evening, I drive to the house where Ceri's mother lived and died.

As soon as I plugged Hannah Tennison's address into my phone's map, it zoomed into one of the most affluent parts of the city. Victoria University's campus sits in the west end of the city and is surrounded by mansions. While Ceri's mother lived in one of the less extravagant homes along Four Cedar Road, it still makes a three bedroom rancher look like a crack house by comparison.

My black Hyundai Elantra grumbles to a stop in the driveway of the gray stone house. I click on the garage door opener sitting in my passenger seat, and the wide, white doors lift open. Just before coming here, I'd stopped by Avalon to pick up the garage door opener and the keys. Ceri had dropped them off with the bartender earlier in the day. I told her the spell I needed to perform tonight required me to avoid any direct contact with the deceased's relatives. That's a lie. After last night, the way I lost control with her, I'm in no hurry to meet with my new client face-to-face again. My better sense hasn't stopped me from thinking on what happened between us. Dammit, I even dreamed about Ceri after I went to bed last night.

Parking inside the garage, I close the garage door. The car next to mine is a silver Jaguar. What on earth did Ceri's mother do for a living? I can't help but think this is inherited wealth, because that's not all that uncommon in this part of town.

The inside of the house doesn't disappoint. The garage leads me into the kitchen, which is pristine. You could safely perform open heart surgery on the granite counters. Hell, you could probably do it on the hardwood floors. I'm wearing a denim jacket, a brown Led Zeppelin t-shirt and blue jeans. For the second time in as many days, I feel underdressed, even though I'm the only living person here.

I make my way through the family room to the master bedroom. "This is disgusting." The bedroom looks just as immaculate as the rest of the house. Did Ceri's mom live here or was she just the curator for this suburban museum?

The queen size, four-poster bed is made of wood with a dark finish. Pulling back the red velvet comforter, I take the pillow that looks like it gets the most use and remove its black pillow case. Red, white, and black dominate the décor, giving this bedroom a cold "Queen of Hearts" vibe. In a minor protest to these exceedingly tidy surroundings, I don't bother to fix the bed sheets.

Did Ceri grow up here? It's hard to imagine her in this place. Everything about her spirit feels so warm and inviting, but her mom's home makes me think her mother's spirit would take offense at my sneakers walking on the white carpet of her bedroom.

I find the rest of what I need in the bathroom. A comb still has some of Hannah's hair. I pull a few of the long, auburn strands from the comb's teeth and put them into the pillow case. A stop by the dirty clothes hamper leads me to an older pair of underwear. I scowl as I pull the dead woman's intimates from the pile and toss them into the pillow case. Summoning the spirit of the recently departed is always an invasive act, no matter how well-intentioned the summoner's motives might be.

I stop back by the kitchen and dig around until I find a large, steel wok.

The stairs to the basement lead me to the laundry room and a large, metal door with a keypad attached. I don't need the code to enter, though. The door is already open, left that way by whoever killed Hannah Tennison.

As soon as I cross the threshold into Hannah's vault, a chill rushes through me. The fact someone was murdered here would normally be enough to unnerve me, but it's more than that. Whatever artifacts she'd kept locked away in here, one or more of them were powerful—more powerful than anything I've ever encountered.

"What the hell were you hiding in here?" With any luck, Hannah's spirit will answer the question.

The floor of the room is black marble. Four white, Roman-style pillars are in the room with nothing on top of them. The walls are painted black with glass display cases that are all shattered open. Hannah's killer didn't leave a single artifact.

Placing the steel wok on the floor, I toss in the personal items I gathered. I sit down on the floor with my legs crossed. I pull a small silver flask from my breast pocket, unscrew the top and take a shot of Espolòn Blanco. I always find if you're going to fuck with someone, its best to do it with tequila. Then I sprinkle some of the tequila onto the items in the wok with a glance skyward to ask forgiveness of the Big Lady above for the waste of good tequila. After I put away the flask, I pull out a box of matches, light one and toss it in.

"Burn, baby, burn."

I get my wish, and it doesn't smell pleasant. The smoke doesn't taste great either, but I need to take it in for this to work. The essence of Hannah in my lungs will make it easier to call on her spirit. Laying on my back, I close my eyes and focus on Hannah.

The smoke moves within my mind. A simple thought grabs onto it and pulls my spirit free of my body. When I open my eyes, I'm standing naked in a smoky void. The wok is there with me, but the flames from it burn pink and green.

I curse under my breath, not that my spirit actually needs to breathe. The pink is a good sign. That means Hannah's spirit is still close. The green, though... That means something far less friendly is nearby. I need to find Hannah fast, and then get off this plane and back into my physical body.

Reaching towards the fire, I tug at the pink flames, careful to avoid the green ones. The pink flames lift free of the wok and spins in a spiral.

"Hannah, can you hear me?"

A pulse ripples up through the spiral of pink flames.

"Hannah Tennison?"

"Yes?" The word echoes from the pink flames as they expand into the shape of a woman. She looks as if she might say more, but then she stares at her arms, as if fascinated by the sight of her body shaped from flames.

"Hannah, do you know where you are?" Some spirits understand they're dead, but others don't. Confront them with the fact they're a ghost, and they might panic.

Her eyes narrow as she looks up at me. She nods, and without a word, she eliminates any doubt she knows exactly where she is and how she got here.

"Why are you here?" she asks.

"The person who killed you stole all of your artifacts. Your daughter hired me to find them. Do you know who took them?"

"My daughter?" Even if I couldn't see the look on her face, the way she says that makes it clear she doesn't trust me.

"I met with Ceri last night."

She crosses her arms. "Did she tell you her full name?"

"Yes, she did." She's testing me, and the way she arches her eyebrow leaves no doubt she's not going to say more until I tell her the name Ceri gave me. "Cerina Alethea Tennison."

Her shoulders relax on the middle name. I'm starting to understand the way her home is. There's a calculated precision to her gestures and words.

"There was something very powerful among the objects taken from your home," I say. "Even days after they were stolen, I can still feel its echo within the room where you kept it. What did they take?"

The way her face shifts through unshared thoughts puzzles me. She almost seems surprised I'm asking this and then concerned. The shifting of her expressions gets ahead of me, partly because of her face being formed from pink flames. I don't miss slump of her shoulders at the end of her internal conversation. That's a look of resignation.

"I don't know."

"Excuse me?" I take a step closer to her. "You owned one of the most powerful magical artifacts I've ever sensed, and you haven't any idea what it is?"

"That wasn't mine."

"Which one?"

"Any of it." She raises her hands in a show of surrender. "None of them belonged to me. I just looked after them."

She was a glorified curator for a private collection, hired for the task. That's kind of funny in light of my earlier thoughts about her home being more like a museum, but I decide it's best not to share that with her. "So who do they belong to?"

She sighs. "I can't tell you that."

"Hannah, you're already dead. Whoever owns those items isn't coming after you."

That snaps her head up to glare at me. "You really think being dead makes me safe. Considering you're here, doesn't that make it clear just how possible another might do the same?"

I can't argue with that, not when she's right. There are certainly ways to harm a soul once it's left the earthly plane.

"Is there a catalog with the items you had in there? Something that can help me know what was taken or find the person who killed you?"

"I don't even know who killed me. She wore a ski mask. All I know is that she was probably white with brown eyes." She shakes her head. "I didn't keep a list of the items in that room. I was paid to look after them, and I failed."

I glance towards the wok, which is mostly green flames with Hannah pulled apart from the fire. Is it my imagination, or is the fire getting more intense? Even if that's my imagination, this is taking too long. I'm lucky my presence here hasn't drawn any unwanted attention yet. There are things on the spiritual plane that would consider the soul of a living being a rare feast.

"What if I describe them for you?" Hannah's question pulls my attention back to her.

"How many items were in that vault?"

"Sixteen."

"We don't have that long. Would you be willing to let me see your memory of the room?"

She steps back. "How do I know you won't take more than that from my thoughts?"

"I can only give you my word and the fact that Ceri is trusting me to recover what was taken."

I could try to offer some sort of argument, but there's nothing that isn't bullshit. She's right in that I could try to take more than the memory she offers. I'd be lying if I didn't admit I was considering doing just that, but I've no guarantee that I won't need to make this trip again to speak with her. If I betray her this time, I'll never get anything out of her during the next visit.

She mutters "Alethea" under her breath and sighs. "Fine. I'll let you pull my memory of the items in the vault."

I step up to her and place my hands within an inch of each side of her head. "I'll be quick about it, and I vow to take no more than that. Please focus on the memory, and let me know when you have it fixed in your thoughts."

She closes her eyes. "I have it."

I touch the sides of her head and close my eyes. For a split second, it's as if I've been thrust back into the vault, but then I see all the items that were missing and the glass cases undamaged.

I hold onto the thought so that it's seared into my own memory, because I'll need to draw all of this once I'm back on the earthly plane.

Just as I think I've got it fixed in my mind, the entire vision is consumed in green flames.

Every nerve in my body explodes, pulling a scream out of me.

I've lingered too long, and the predators I'd feared have found

Chapter 2: Echoes

us.

Chapter 3: Enfer à Trois

My vision snaps free of Hannah's memory. It's worse than I'd feared.

The green flames had suggested a succubus wraith, but I've drawn not only one of them but two. They aren't true succubi, but what they want and what they do are close enough for Wikipedia purposes.

Unlike Hannah, whose spirit is only flames, these wraiths have a more physical form. They have green skin with long, black hair and are adorned in bright green flames. One is pressed to my back, arms snaking around my chest and stomach. The other pushes Hannah aside to cup my face in her hands. Their touch burns pleasure into my spirit, and the jolt to my system is paralyzing, making it impossible fight back with any success. The best I manage is to flail in their grip.

"Hannah, go!" They aren't interested in her yet, but if I escape or if these wraiths consume me, they'll move onto her next. With a gesture, I cast Hannah back into the fire. The pink flames burn there for a moment before they vanish. That leaves only the green flames in the wok, and I suspect the two succubus wraiths are just the first of many more.

As long as they hold me, I can't escape, not without pulling one of them out into the earthly plane. Even worse, they'd possess me like a parasite, and if I didn't rid myself of them soon enough, they'd become a permanent part of me, transforming me into someone completely different: a sort of living death.

Knowing all that doesn't stop my spirit's form from betraying me, though. The one behind me reaches down between my legs, and my eyes roll back in my head as my legs give out. The succubus wraiths pull me to the ground. I should fight to get up, but all I can do is spread my legs to give the wraith's fingers all the access they desire. The way her fingers dip inside my cunt quicken my memory of Ceri fingering me to climax in Avalon and the dreams I had of her all last night after that.

"She wants her," the wraith caressing my face says.

I open my eyes. Her black hair loses its curls, straightening to match Ceri's style, including the length that had reached down to the middle of her back. The succubus even changes her face. Other than the green skin and the eyes that are nothing but seas of bright green fire, the shape is a perfect match to Ceri's.

"She can have her," the other wraith says, moving in front of me with her hand still pleasuring me between my legs. She's also transformed into a green Ceri.

"No," I gasp, even though my hips buck with joy.

The one touching my face leans in to kiss me. When her dark lips press against mine, my mouth welcomes hers. The flames playing across her skin also dance across her tongue. She tastes like the spiciest and sweetest peppermint I've ever known. As the kiss deepens, her fire fills my spirit, burning off a part of it from within and then sucking out the ashes. I swoon from the sensation, an instant high.

I whimper as I feel the fingers of the other succubus teasing my cunt pull away. Both her hands then push my legs even farther apart. When her tongue traces the edges of my pussy lips, the fingers are quickly forgotten. I moan into the kiss of the first succubus wraith as the other sucks on my clitoris. She's too skilled and too clever, quickly figuring out exactly how I best enjoy having someone go down on me.

There's no fighting it at this point, and when I cum, my entire body quakes with joy. Heat fills me as the flames from their tongues collide in me near my heart.

A split second of sanity in the afterglow shocks sense back into me. I need to cast them back into the fire, the same as I did with Hannah. Only Hannah was willing, the succubus wraiths are determined to stay and feast.

I break from the kiss of the first wraith and glare up at her. Her eyes widen in panic as my thoughts form the incantation and rip her off of me. She screams as she's flung back into the fire. An instinctive panic gets the better of me. I know she isn't Ceri, but the sight of Ceri's face, no matter the hue, contorted into fear catches me off guard. I've only known her for one day, but the idea of her being harmed by me, knowing that's what her face would look like, startles me.

I'm a fool, because then something pinches my nipple. Pain and pleasure ignite within my breast. The remaining wraith gropes my breasts and periodically tweaks my nipples. The blissful distraction leaves me all too willing to lie there and succumb to all of the pleasures this wraith can offer.

She continues her oral assault. I grab her hair and pull her tongue deep against my cunt. I want to cum again. I mumble and gasp my need as I feel the next wave drawing close.

I scream to the Goddess as I cum again. The succubus wraith's flames fill me once more, and a small part of me realizes the only reason I'm alive is because I expelled the first succubus wraith. My heart stutters, and even though it's only a spiritual representation of my heart, I know the threat to my continued life is very real.

With all the energy I have left, I jerk on the wraith's hair to pull her away from my dripping cunt. She growls in protest as she fights my grip on her hair. She grabs onto my wrist, but in doing so, her hands stop playing with my body.

I scream as I force my thoughts to form the incantation and send the succubus wraith to join the other in the fire.

Even as I do, I see a third succubus wraith's arm reach out of the wok's fire and her glowing eyes of fire staring out at me. I won't survive another one.

I reach up and scream again as I use all of my remaining willpower to pierce the veil of the spiritual plane and restore myself to my physical body.

Then it all goes dark and cold.

Chapter 4: Artifacts

It's almost eleven by the time I park my car in the alley behind the Solstice Bookstore. I grab my sketch pad and a heavy, white paper bag from my passenger seat before I climb out and ascend the wooden stairs to the second floor porch.

I knock on the turquoise, wooden door. Footsteps from within the apartment stalk up to the door, followed by the bolt sliding and the door cracking open with a chain still barring me entry. Also keeping me at bay is the scowl of a familiar set of blue eyes behind a pair of circular wire rim frames.

"You realize what time it is?"

I hold up the paper bag, giving it a little shake to demonstrate just how full it is. Kelly has a soft spot for red velvet cookies, especially the ones from the Full Moon Cookie Shop. It's a hole-in-the-wall bakery that's only open at night and caters mostly to the downtown college crowd. During midterms and finals, the place stays open all the way to sunrise for the students who are cramming and need the sugar rush. I made sure to stop there on my way from Hannah Tennison's.

Kelly groans in disgust as she closes the door, but then I hear the chain latch clinking as she undoes it and opens the door wide for me to enter.

"You never come here unless you want something, so what is it?" She brushes a stray strand of her shoulder-length hair out of her face. She's had it dyed dark blue for about a year now and looks as if she got it touched up within the past few days.

I stroll in, handing over the bag of goodies. "I did text you I was coming."

She moans with delight as she cracks open the bag and inhales the perfume of freshly baked cookies. "I keep my phone off at night, which you know."

She shuts the door as I walk down the narrow hallway that leads past her bedroom and to the living room. Getting through the hallway requires turning sideways, because the walls are lined with bookshelves. The living room is also wall-to-wall bookshelves, all of which are overflowing.

Kelly storms past me, clutching the bag of cookies to her chest, and goes into the kitchen where she sets them on the counter. "You know, you could actually visit sometimes instead of only bugging me every time you need something."

I laugh as I lean against the door frame to her kitchen. "Just because I'd be visiting doesn't mean I wouldn't be wanting something from you." She's wearing a Union Jack t-shirt tonight, and it's hugging so tightly to her chest that I'm in danger of becoming an anglophile.

She grabs her kettle and fills it with water. "Girl, you gotta earn this, and by my accounting, you're too far in my debt to ever have me owing you a thing."

"Feel free to collect."

She talks a good game, but the playful grin over her shoulder ruins her attempt at annoyance with me. "Leaded?" she asks as she pulls a can of cinnamon churro coffee from her pantry.

"Yes, please."

"You're looking like shit, Monica."

"Oo... Flattery will get you everywhere."

"Please, if I even suggested you could do the horizontal mambo with me, you'd dive into my bed wearing nothing but a pair of sparkly red dancing shoes." Her expression turns serious as she scoops the coffee into her French press. "Seriously, what are you into?"

We go out into the living room while we wait for the water to boil. A dark brown, wooden coffee table with three piles of books, one of which has toppled, sits in the middle of the room between a pair of fainting chairs. Kelly sprawls across the purple velvet seat, leaving the teal velvet chair for me to lie on. I've crashed a few times on this one over the years.

"A pair of succubus wraiths got the drop on me earlier tonight while I was communing with a murder victim."

She scowls at me. "That's uncommonly sloppy of you."

I ignore her, mainly because I know she's right, and flip open my sketch pad. "Someone murdered my client's mother and stole more than a dozen magical objects from her vault."

Handing Kelly the sketch pad, she flips through my drawings of what I saw in Hannah's memory. She mutters to herself as he goes through them. "A sacrificial dagger, a cloak that probably claims invisibility, a crystal skull, no clue what that is, or that. Some kind of ceremonial cup. Except for the skull and the scimitar, most of this looks Greek in origin."

"Yeah, there are about six items in there I don't have a clue what they do or why they might be important."

The kettle whistles, drawing Kelly up off her chair. She drops the sketch pad on her coffee table as she strolls into the kitchen. "Most of it looks like expensive junk."

"At least one of the items in there is the real deal," I call to her without getting up. "Even though the murder and theft happened five days ago, the vault was still flooded with magical energy."

"Your client tell you what was taken?" I can hear her pouring the water into the French press and then fiddling around with some coffee mugs.

"She doesn't know. Her mother never said what was in there, only that it was important for her to guard the vault if anything ever happened to her."

The kitchen goes quiet. I turn to see Kelly standing in the doorway staring at me over the rims of her glasses.

"What?" I ask.

"She?"

"She's just a client." Just a client I fucked in a private booth, but no way I'm confessing that to the sexiest bookseller on the east coast.

"Uh huh," Kelly says in that way that translates into "Bullshit." She turns back into the kitchen to finish getting the coffee together.

I bang my head against the cushioned back of the chair I'm lounging on.

"Well," Kelly says while digging out a small container of heavy cream from her fridge, "I doubt any of the items I recognize would generate the amount of magical energy you're describing."

"But you'd be willing to dig around to see what the rest of those items might be?" I say, gesturing to her many bookshelves.

She walks back into her living room and sets a dark blue mug of coffee in front of me. I don't bother asking what she's added, because Kelly figured out a long time ago I prefer my coffee with cream and no sugar. She takes hers with cream and a small bit of raw sugar.

"I might be willing." She places the bag of cookies on the coffee table on her side, just out of my reach. She reclines on her purple velvet chair as she eyes me. "Just how do you plan to make it worth my while, because the cookies are good, but they aren't that good?"

We trade playful expressions through the steam from our coffee mugs.

"Oh, I might be willing to pay for your services, but I am a little tight on money."

Kelly taps the rim of her mug as her eyes roam over me. "I can think of a few things you might do for me, but you aren't going to get that lucky tonight."

"Tease."

"You're one to talk. One day I'm going to call your bluff, and my money says you'll chicken out."

I sip my coffee. "Well, my money says you'll never get the nerve to call my bluff."

"You mean the money you don't have?" Kelly laughs.

"That's harsh."

"But accurate."

I sigh. "Well, that's why I need to close this case fast."

Her eyes linger on me, and I like the way they do. It's as if Kelly could grope me with her thoughts. Fifteen years ago, we met in college in what turned into a one night stand. Then five years ago, I wandered into her bookstore downstairs with one of my moms, who was hunting for a specific book of the arcane. Kelly and I recognized each other instantly, but neither of us said a thing with my mother there. I came back the next day. We caught up over coffee at one of the local cafes, but nothing beyond friendship occurred. Ever since, we've been doing this awkward dance, as if damned to make up for all the chaste courtship we failed to do that first night. It's more than that, though. Kelly is my best friend, and I like to think I'm hers. The idea of potentially losing that terrifies me, because when your list of exes is as long as mine, there's a point at which you have to accept you're the problem.

"Fortunately for you, I'm not working tomorrow. I've got Selena handling the store, so I'll see what I can find for you."

We catch up on other things, mostly book recommendations and local gossip. She's shorthanded in the bookstore, because she had to fire one of her booksellers for being perpetually late. The three times the cops had to come to the store, because she got into domestic arguments while on the clock didn't help matters. Kelly also mentions she's car shopping, which she hates more than cilantro (she has a serious hate on for cilantro that I've never understood).

"You need to go with me when I do the test drive," she says around a mouthful of red velvet cookie.

"Why? You know how to negotiate with a car dealer better than I do."

"Yes, but I'm less likely to kill the condescending shit and end up in jail if you're there to stop me."

Sensing my negotiating position with Kelly has improved, I sit up and reach over to snag a cookie from the bag on her side of the coffee table. "This is true."

"And I wouldn't object to you doing a little," she pauses to wiggle her fingers in the air, not that I ever wiggle my fingers like that when I cast a spell. "You know—to help me get a better price."

I sit up and place my hand to my chest in mock horror. "I would never do anything that unethical."

We both laugh, and Kelly's smile makes me want to climb on her and rip off that Union Jack shirt. Once she's stopped laughing, her gaze slides over me. My whole body tingles, because I think she wants me to act on my lust. Instead, I lean back and sip my coffee.

She's right about me. I'm too chicken to make the move.

"I should go. Going to need to run down some leads in the morning."

Kelly doesn't move to stand. She just stares up at me as if to silently say, *I told you so, you coward.*

"You sure you're safe to drive?" Her concern is sincere, but I can't help but wonder if there's more than that in there, an invitation to stay and share a different kind of dessert with her legs wrapped around my head.

Only it's not Kelly's legs in my imagination. It's Ceri's.

"I'll be fine. Thanks for the help, but you get some rest, too."

We waste no time finishing our goodbyes. I have to force myself not to race out her door and down the stairs to where I parked my car. Once I'm sitting in the driver's seat, I let out a long breath. I can't help but feel like the worst kind of friend, flirting with Kelly while fantasizing about another woman.

Why can't I shake Ceri from my mind? I think about last night, how everyone in Avalon was so overly amorous. Was that why we both lost control? Something influencing everyone? Or was Ceri manipulating me? What worries me most is that if the answer to the last question is "yes," then I'm not sure that's enough to stop me from wanting to be with her again.

Chapter 5: Talk Dirty to Me

The next day finds me in a foul mood.

Getting to sleep last night was almost impossible. Between nearly getting consumed by the succubus wraiths, ogling Kelly's Union Jack-wrapped boobs, and my guilt and questions about Ceri, my mind wouldn't shut down for anything. I finally resorted to two shots of tequila and a furious ride on my favorite vibrator. After my fourth orgasm, while desperately screaming and babbling Ceri's name the entire time, I managed to pass out.

A raging headache greeted me around ten in the morning. Two mugs of coffee helped ease the pain, but didn't do anything for my pussy, which was raw from the rough treatment I gave myself last night.

My ill temperament helps when I go to Vonda's pawn shop. There are plenty of pawn shops in the city, but for anyone who knows anything about mystical artifacts, Vonda's is really the only place to go. Doesn't take long for Vonda to give me what I need to know: the woman who pawned the items stolen from

Hannah's vault.

This time, I make the extra effort to look my best, because Vonda gave me plenty of insight into the thief who killed Hannah. "Gina's one kinky bitch. Really short and constantly feels the need to compensate for it, like a tiny dog that thinks it can intimidate a Doberman if she barks at it enough. She's a real anime nut, too. Loves her girls meek and with colorful hair."

More importantly, Vonda gave me Gina's address.

Gina lives in one of the newer, cookie cutter apartment buildings that have sprung up throughout downtown during the past couple years. The fifth floor reeks of marijuana as soon as I step off the elevator.

I stroll up to apartment 508 and knock hard on the door. The door cracks open, and one light brown eye glares out at me. Dialogue in what I assume is Japanese erupts from her apartment.

"What do you want?" Even though she barks out the question in a threatening tone, the way she looks at me changes almost instantly.

Her gaze goes first to my hair. I put on a neon blue wig of straight hair that goes down to my ass. My outfit is hidden beneath a black trench coat, but I'm wearing it open enough to show off plenty of cleavage.

I grin back at her, because she obviously likes what she sees. The door opens wider to reveal she's probably about five foot three with wavy brown hair down to her shoulders that's got that messy look to it that's just too perfect to not be intentional.

"I'm Penelope." I bite my bottom lip as I untie the belt of my trench coat, pulling it open to reveal what I'm not wearing. My hot pink, off the shoulder top is pulled down enough to make it obvious I'm not wearing a bra. The black leather miniskirt also doesn't hurt to grab her attention. "You must be Donna, apartment 708?" I keep my gaze downcast to avoid looking her in the eyes, as I sway in place, right to left. "You paid for two hours, right?"

It's a weak gambit. It might not normally work, but I didn't just play dress-up for this encounter. I spent the previous hour cultivating a seduction spell. I could have shown up in a t-shirt and jeans, and Gina would've been gagging for it. That I've dressed to her tastes while acting the part of the sub makes me a morsel she can't resist.

"Well," Gina says with a purr to the word, "get on in here."

I answer in a hushed voice. "Yes, ma'am."

As soon as I'm through the door, I'm weaving a spell on Gina. Despite my joking with Kelly last night, I don't like to use my magic to manipulate others, but I'm not feeling any hesitation with the woman who most likely killed Ceri's mother. While I could crush Gina's will in one strike, it's a risky move that usually only works on a willing victim. Even without Vonda's description of Gina, I can smell the dom on her. She wouldn't give into me without a fight, and if she has any magical talent or some mystical quality I've not sussed out yet, she might realize what I'm doing and attack.

The apartment isn't what I expected. That it's a studio apartment doesn't shock me, but it's disturbingly tidy. The kitchen runs along the left wall without a stain on the white countertop nor a dish in the sink. A large plasma TV playing an anime I don't recognize with the subtitles on is mounted on the wall just past the kitchen. The main room of the apartment has a dark purple, leather sofa. The bed is set against the far wall and is made up with a military precision to the black comforter and grey pillows. A picture of a techno-thriller-style skyline hangs over the headboard. The door to a small balcony sits open, letting in a pleasant breeze.

"Where would you like me, ma'am?" I ask as I let my trench coat drop to the floor by her sofa.

Gina leans back against the counter at the edge of the kitchen and seethes with lust as she takes in my appearance. I can tell she's digging the black, thigh-high boots I'm wearing. "Not ma'am." She marches over to me and traces a finger down my jawline. "I want you to address me as 'My Queen.'"

"Yes, my Queen." I keep my gaze down, focused on her waist.

The belt to her black pants has a silver buckle shaped like a butterfly. Her top is a grey, ribbed tank top that clings to her small chest.

She strolls around me, her hand tracing a possessive path along my torso.

"Just what does my two hours get me?"

I whisper back to her. "My body belongs to you, my Queen. My safe word is puppy."

The safe word pulls a smile out of her. "Stay right here, servant."

"Yes, my Queen."

She walks around the sofa and picks her remote off the arm of the chair. Clicking the buttons, she changes the TV to play a trip hop playlist set to a psychedelic visualizer. She drops the remote back onto the arm of the sofa and walks back to me.

"Lean over the back of the couch."

"Yes, my Queen." I do as I'm told and arch my back to push my ass high up, giving her a hint of my bright blue thong, underwear.

Pain explodes through my bottom as her hand cracks against

my ass. "Your coat doesn't belong on the floor."

"Yes, my Queen," I shriek as a second blow lands on my bottom. I stand to get the coat off the floor, but she shoves me back down.

"I didn't say to move, servant!"

"Yes, my Queen." I lean back over the sofa and cry out again as she spanks me even harder than the first two times. I wiggle my ass for her. "You have such a strong hand and a sexy voice."

I suspect the prompt about her voice would normally draw an angry protest out of her, but my magic is working on her. Her heavy breathing makes it clear she's getting turned on fast.

"Fold your coat, servant, and take off your skirt. Put them on the bed."

"Yes, my Queen."

When I stand, she's walking away instead of watching me. She disappears into the bathroom for a moment. I hear her rummaging through a drawer as I unzip my skirt and slip it off. I use the brief moment I'm alone to study her home without hiding my intentions. Nothing about the apartment suggests she owns any mystical artifacts. If she has the few items that weren't in Vonda's shop, then she's got them hidden well, most likely somewhere else. Vonda didn't have the powerful one I could still sense while in Hannah's vault, and I'm not sensing it in Gina's apartment.

"Very good, servant."

I look up from where I left my folded coat and skirt to see Gina standing naked by her sofa. She licks her lips as she takes in my ass, probably admiring the red mark where she spanked me.

"Go stand on the balcony and dance for me."

I'm tempted to break out the safe word, but it's too soon. I'm

39

still weaving my will around hers. Much like any other spell, it's a matter of deliberate thought. Before coming here, I ate a piece of chocolate and drank a small glass of red wine. The items I consumed don't matter, not exactly. The incantation requires me to eat the things I most closely associate with sex, the more decadent, the better. I wrapped my body in that idea of sex, and that's why Gina couldn't resist me at the door. Now, I'm unspooling the thread of that idea and weaving it around her, only where I wore the thread like lingerie, I'm methodically tying it around her like a rope to leash her.

"Yes, my Queen." I walk over to the door to the balcony, making a show of swaying my hips. "The more you speak, the more I obey."

My thread of seduction is wrapped around her wrists now.

I sway to the music as I step out onto her balcony. I hold onto the top of the door frame and cling to it as I dance, letting her soak in the sight of my body's curves.

"Yes," Gina hisses. "Like that, servant."

She climbs onto the back of her sofa, straddling it. The grinding sound of a small vibrator springs to life. She takes turns rubbing against the vibrator and the back of her sofa. Her eyes never leave me.

"Keep dancing, servant." She groans, close to reaching her orgasm, what she probably assumes will be the first of many. "Take off the fucking shirt. I want your tits out."

"Yes, my Queen. Your voice guides me." Even though I have my wig pinned on, I'm careful not to pull it off as I slip out of my top.

She grunts as she grinds more furiously against the vibrator. "Fuck yes!"

I chuckle as I tighten my mystical leash around her wrists and legs. The effect is instantaneous.

"You want more, my Queen?"

Hooded eyes look up at me as she pants. "Stay there and keep dancing, but lose the underwear."

Dammit. She isn't quite hooked in yet, but the fact she didn't call me "servant" that time shows I'm starting to get her where I need her.

I give her another good view of my ass as I slip out of my thong, leaving me naked for all to see with only my thigh high boots still on.

Gina rocks hard against the back of her sofa. The nipples of her small breasts are rock hard. With her free hand, she pinches one of them.

"Fuck, fuck, fuck!" She draws circles with her vibrator around her bud. Her scream is muffled as she bites down on the inside of her arm.

She's gasping for air as I finish the last loop of the magical thread, this time around her throat, and tighten it. There's no missing the change in her eyes. The cruelty vanishes, replaced with wide-eyed amazement.

"It feels so good to talk to me." I walk back into her apartment and grip her by the throat. "Doesn't it, my Queen?" I give the honorific a cruel twist, because she's no longer the one in control here, not that she ever really was.

"Yes, it feels so good to talk to you." She's still riding hard against the back of her sofa as I grip her neck harder and pull her to me.

"That's right, my Queen, and you want to tell me anything I want to know."

"Anything." She gasps out the word.

"And everything."

"Yes, yes… and everything."

I push her down onto her back. She's still trying to hump her furniture, but the angle is all wrong now. I yank the vibrator out her hand and then glide it along her vulva.

"Are you a thief, my Queen?"

Her eyes roll back in her head as I tighten my grip on her throat. I have to stop myself from choking her, though, so she can still answer.

"Yes." Her hips buck against the vibrator in my hand.

"That's right, my Queen. Talking to me and telling me the truth feels better than anything you've ever known."

"Oh, fuck me! Yes! Yes! Fuck, yes!" She screams as she cums.

"Very good, my Queen. Now tell me, did you steal from a woman's home in the west end last week?"

"I did." She smiles like she's just done something deserving a reward, eager to please me so I'll keep playing with her pussy.

"Did you kill her, my Queen?"

I do choke her then, and she cums even harder than before. My better sense asserts itself, and I loosen my grip. She speaks in a ragged voice. "I did. Killed her. Yes, yes."

"Why!" I shove her down onto the sofa cushions and keep her pinned there with both of my hands around her throat. "Why did you kill her?"

By now, she's loving it too much to fight. She's got her hands between her legs and is shoving her fingers into her dripping wet snatch. "I was paid to!" She shouts the confession in a cry of bliss.

Paid? What the fuck?

"Who? Who paid you!"

"Anessa! Anessa!" She shrieks the name as she keeps finger fucking herself.

"Anessa Kotov?" Please don't let Gina say it's her.

"Yes!"

I let go of her and stumble back. I start to fall, but I grab onto the balcony door in time to stop myself.

"Wait!" Gina is sitting up on her knees on the sofa with her hand still fingering her swollen pussy, eager for for me to make her cum again. "I'll tell you anything else you like. I love telling you things! Anything!"

I think of Ceri, how I told her I wouldn't kill for her, but I know it's going to break her heart when she learns her mother was murdered by some common thief, a thief who was paid to do it.

"Why did Anessa have you do it? What did she want?"

Gina hops up and down on her hand as she nods to me. "She wanted the crown. Gave it to her. Let me. Let me. Oh, fuck! Let me keep the rest!"

Her head lolls back as she climaxes, her juices running down the inside of her thighs.

"Where are the artifacts you didn't pawn to Vonda?"

She whimpers, unable to stop herself from masturbating. "Beneath... Under... floor in my... closet!"

"You want me to make you feel more pleasure, you fucking bitch?" I'm done pretending she has any control left.

She nods and grins to me as she rubs in desperation for another orgasm. "Yes, please, please, please. I'll tell you anything."

"That's a good bitch."

"I am. Such a good fucking bitch for you!"

I laugh. So much for the little dom.

"Then you're going to call the police, confess to killing that woman, and give them the artifacts you've stashed in your floor.

You won't tell them you did it for Anessa Kotov, though. That you keep to yourself. You did it all yourself. That's what you'll tell them."

"Yes! I'm good at telling things!"

"Call the police now!"

She hops off the sofa and runs into the bathroom to get her phone.

As I hear her babbling to the 911 dispatcher, I get dressed and leave. I stumble down the hallway, dizzy as if I was the one who'd just had the orgasm marathon.

Anessa Kotov.

I've never met her—praise the Goddess! But I'm all too familiar with Anessa's reputation. She's one of the most powerful people in the city's magical underworld.

Chapter 6: Delivering the News

I sit in my car in the parking garage across from my apartment building for about a half hour debating on calling Ceri. I need to call her, because there's no excuse for her to learn about the thief's confession from the police before I've talked to her. I can't decide exactly what to tell her, though. The truth is dangerous. I've at least found her mother's killer and most of the items that were stolen.Vonda gave me her word she plans to hand over the items to the police.

The problem is that one item not recovered. That means unanswered questions.

Questions Ceri will obviously ask.

I don't see a way to tell her that without letting her know someone hired her mother's killer, that someone wanted her mother dead. There are good reasons not to tell her. The most important reason being that she shouldn't cross a woman like Anessa Kotov.

The problem is that I'd be lying to Ceri. I can't stomach the idea she might later realize I've deceived her. It shouldn't matter that much.

She's just a client.

Right.

I've never gotten that intimate with a client.

Okay, that's not entirely true. I have, but it's always been after the case was finished.

Except that one time.

I mean, three times, but still.

Goddess above and below, I really am the problem.

"Fuck it."

I dial Ceri's number.

"Monica?" Hearing her say my name sends a bizarre thrill and chill through me all at once. I suddenly realize the succubus wraiths had imitated her voice, too, but I'd been too distracted to recognize it at the time.

"I hope I'm not calling too late, but I have some news."

I glance at the display on my car's clock. It's almost ten o'clock.

"You don't sound like it's good news." There's no missing the way that's a question.

"It's complicated." I'm screaming on the inside, because I know I've just guaranteed I have to come clean on everything... maybe.

"Maybe it's best if you come here then." The way she says that makes me dizzy, and when I don't answer, she quickly adds, "If you're okay doing that. I just don't know that I'm comfortable doing this over the phone."

"I'm okay with that." Oh, I'm such a fucking liar, unless Merriam-Webster has recently redefined "okay" to mean "completely uncomfortable."

She gives me her address, and I drive to her place. Doesn't take long, because she's in one of the nicer apartment buildings downtown. This time of night, I don't have to worry about parking meters.

If I needed any more evidence that Ceri comes from money, then her apartment settles the matter. She's located on the top floor. Hers is one of only two penthouses. This one smells much nicer than Gina's. The hallway outside the elevator has a circular fountain with the statue of a swan, its wings spread wide as if in flight and spraying water from its mouth.

When I knock on the door, Ceri pulls it open almost immediately.

She starts at the sight of me and the way she grins at me makes me feel as if she's just heard a joke that I don't understand.

"Did you dye your hair?" she asks.

Fuck me. I was so panicked about what to tell Ceri and then about meeting her, it didn't even occur to me I'm still dressed up like some anime girl wet dream.

"Sorry, I was dressed like this, because…" I stand there and struggle for any words to come to mind. The best I manage is, "This is a disguise."

"It's a good look." Her smile widens, and she pulls open the door for me to come inside. "Would you like me to take your coat?"

I stop just inside her apartment. Her apartment is massive, and it is gorgeous. The hardwood floor shines. She has a dark brown leather sofa with two matching chairs around a dark green marble coffee table.

The open floor plan also shows an amazing kitchen that reminds me a bit of her mother's mansion, but it's warmer. There's even a glass vase of red roses on the dining room table.

I'm so busy taking in her apartment that I take a moment to realize Ceri is talking.

"Monica? Did you want me to take your coat?"

"Sure." I slip it off without thinking.

Ceri is biting her bottom lip as she looks at my outfit. This is humiliating. I should have kept the coat on.

"Exactly what kind of disguise were you going for?" She doesn't bother concealing her amusement from her voice.

I let out a long sigh, my head drooping forward to look at her feet instead of her face. "Honestly? Anime call girl."

"I'd say you nailed it."

I look up in time to see her blush as she hangs my coat on a dark wooden hangar and places in it in her entry closet.

"Would you like some wine? I've got a bottle of Riesling already chilled." She leans against the door to the closet as she looks at me again. I can't decide if she's laughing at me or ogling me, and I'm equally uncertain which I'd prefer. I'm certainly ogling her, because she's wearing a dark green, satin halter top that her breasts fill out in the most spectacular fashion. The v-neck front seems to invite me in closer, and I want to answer that call on my knees. The black midi skirt she's wearing is equally inviting, high slit up to the top of her right thigh where the fabric is knotted, creating the illusion that a single tug might undo the knot and send it floating to the floor.

Realizing she's waiting for me to answer her question, I whisper, "Wine sounds perfect."

As Ceri strolls over to the kitchen, I realize she's barefoot. She gestures me towards the open glass door to her balcony.

"Just wait outside. I'll join you in a moment."

I walk out onto the balcony, concerned I'll be cold, but I needn't have worried. The balcony is covered and has a fire pit burning in the middle of it. The only place to sit is a pair of black chaise lounge chairs.

My mind struggles to keep anything clear. I'm reminded of how much I'd had home-court advantage at Avalon, and now Ceri has me off-balance.

I keep going back to her outfit. Surely she doesn't lounge around her home like that. I want to fancy she's dressed up for me, but then I think it might be for someone else. Was she on a date? Or is she going to leave here to go on one after I update her on what's happened? It's not that I'm jealous. Am I?

Ceri and my encounter with Gina are sending my mind to places it shouldn't go. I'm also thinking about the succubus wraiths that had adopted Ceri's appearance and voice. Would her mouth feel just as good with her tongue stroking my cunt, the way the wraith had? Then I imagine being naked and straddling the back of that leather sofa for Ceri the way I'd made Gina do it for me. Even after last night's masturbatory marathon, I'm seriously considering excusing myself into her bathroom to make myself cum and hopefully clear my head.

When I turn around to go back inside, I realize it's too late. Ceri walks up to me with two glasses of white wine in her hands. I take the one offered to me, gripping it by the base of its bowl. The chill of the wine creeps through the glass into my fingertips.

"I appreciate you coming to see me." Ceri sips her wine, her eyes locked on mine. "I hope you're not too cold."

I bring my glass to my lips for a sip, but I end up emptying half of its contents. "No, the fire has it comfortable out here."

That and compared to standing naked on Gina's tiny balcony earlier in the night, this is much more pleasant. The view from her balcony is unchallenged, because it's atop a hill overlooking the Boleyn River. A park rests across the river, and at this hour, it's all but empty. The rest of the world seems to be asleep.

"Let's sit." She sets her drink on a small, cube-shaped glass table between the lounge chairs.

I take the other chair. The design and positioning of the seat would make it easy to avoid looking at her, but I don't want to. When she sits, the slit in her skirt reveals most of her toned leg. No, I can't look away. Wouldn't dare to.

"I found your mother's killer."

I don't know why I blurt that out. Perhaps, I just need to be done with it. A voice in the back of my mind tells me she'll lose all interest in me now that I've said that.

The announcement rattles her. Her smile evaporates and her gaze turns out towards the horizon. Her jaw clenches. She nods, but it's a tense movement. The way her unfocused eyes keep shifting about, she's still sifting through all of her thoughts.

She eventually clears her throat and turns to look at me. "What happened?"

"She's confessing to the police."

Warmth fills my chest as I see a thin smile appear on her lips. I want to comfort her, and I wasn't sure even this news would be sufficient for that.

Then she sits up and her head tilts as she realizes how much I haven't told her. "Why did she agree to confess?"

I brush some loose strands of the blue wig back over my shoulder. "Let's just say I provided some incentive. She was calling 911 as I left her apartment and quite giddy about it."

We trade glances for a moment between sips of wine.

"I found her because she'd pawned most of the items to a shop owner I know."

"Most of the items?"

I nod. "There's one item unaccounted for, and I'm not sure getting it back will be as simple as finding your mother's killer was."

"I'm glad you found her killer." She eyes her near empty glass, sets it on the glass table, and stands. "I'm going to get the bottle."

The way most of her leg is exposed, the high slit just short of revealing that warm place between her thighs leaves me speechless as I watch her move.

I turn to the fire, watching the flames dance. They seem to taunt me with what I haven't told Ceri yet. I down the rest of the wine in my glass.

The glubbing sound of wine pouring into Ceri's glass alerts me that she's returned.

"More?"

I hold up my glass for her, and she fills it more liberally this time. We clink our glasses together without either of us making an actual toast.

She reclines on her chair again, and the sight of her leg slipping out of that skirt is just as intoxicating as it was the first time. But then she offers me something more to see. She bends her leg up to rest her foot flat on the lounge chair and it pushes the part of her skirt all the way to that tempting knot. My heart is pounding, and in my distraction, I'm chugging my wine again instead of sipping it.

I set the glass on the small table between us to force myself to slow down, because I can tell I'm buzzing a bit, a pleasant dizziness that makes me want to just stay here and drowse or perhaps to crawl over to Ceri and bury my face between her legs.

Dammit. I need to finish what I came here to do.

"You seem troubled." Ceri cants her head, those deep blue eyes studying me. "What is it you're worried about telling me?"

I can't do this reclining on this lounge chair, so I sit up and turn to face her. The sudden movement makes me realize just how fast the wine really has hit me. My head swims a moment. Once I'm still long enough for my mind to catch up, I get to the matter at hand.

"The thief? She was hired by someone."

"Why—?" She can't finish the question, probably not even sure how to ask it. Doesn't matter, because no matter the question, the answer will be the same.

"Have you ever heard of Anessa Kotov?" The way Ceri's slender eyebrows push in towards each other answers the question for me. "She's a powerful woman in the city's mystical underworld."

"And she's the one who hired this thief?"

I nod. "I don't know why, though. Could be the purpose of the theft was to cover the actual motive for killing your mother or could be the other way around."

"Well, at least the thief's confession will implicate her." Ceri raises her glass and then takes a sip in morbid celebration.

"No, she won't. It wouldn't matter if she did. Anessa Kotov is the Queen Dragon of the city, and the police won't be able to do a thing to her. She is that powerful."

The way Ceri bolts up to her feet, she looks like she might grab a spear to go after Anessa Kotov herself.

I stand, as well. This time, I'm smart enough not to do it as quickly. Damn wine.

"So is this it? This," she pauses waving her hand in the air as she tries to recall Anessa's title, "this Queen Dragon gets away with having my mother killed and stealing whatever it is she's taken?"

I walk over to her and touch her bare arm. Her skin feels deliciously warm to my fingers, and against my better judgment, I lightly grip her. "Not necessarily. It's possible Anessa Kotov has nothing to do with any of this. It could be the thief only believes Anessa was the one hiring her. I plan to go ask Anessa myself."

"She'd actually admit to being involved?" Even if I couldn't see the look on her face, her words are drowning in skepticism.

"As powerful as she is, she has no reason to lie." Now that we're standing this close, I realize Ceri is just a little taller than I am. The more I stare at her, the more distracted I get, and the feel of her skin has me eager to feel more of her body. My voice is hushed as I speak. "Once I've spoken with her, I'll let you know what I've learned."

When she answers, her voice comes out just as soft as mine. "Thank you."

We stand there with my hand still holding her arm. I want to pull her closer, kiss her, and see if that skirt really will come off as easily it seems to promise.

Despite the wine whipping up my lust, I take a deep breath and take a step back, letting go of her. "I can tell you're planning to go out, so I shouldn't keep you."

Her downcast eyes avoid mine. "I wasn't planning to go anywhere."

"Oh, well, I mean, I'm assuming you probably just got back in then, I'll just let you..."

"No." She bites her bottom lip again. The way she does it makes me want to nibble on it, too. "I haven't been anywhere tonight."

She retrieves her wine glass and shakes out her long hair as she takes a step back and sips her wine. "I have a confession. I changed into this, because I knew you were coming over."

The way I'm grinning at her admission must make me look like a foolish school girl, but I can't repress it. The idea she wanted to dress up for me. I wish so badly I'd done the same for her. She looks like a goddess, and I look more suited for a street corner.

She still doesn't want to meet my eyes, her gaze cast downward. "What happened the night we met? I can't stop thinking about it." She does meet my eyes then, and her gaze is as vulnerable as it is hungry. "The way you made me feel, the way you—controlled me. I've never experienced anything like that."

"I didn't mean for that happen." As much as the memory of that night gets me hot and wet between the legs, I feel awful about it. "I shouldn't have let that happen."

She tilts up her wine glass downing all that's left in it. Then she steps close enough that only our breath is between us. "Could you do it again?"

Her fingertips trace along my jawline so that we can't avoid each other's gazes.

"Please," she whispers to me. Her luscious tongue wets her lips. In a breathy voice, she pleads. "Could you do it again? Take it even further?"

I'm not sure how long I stare at her. All I know is that my heart might burst out of my chest. Her fingers make my face tingle in the most wonderful way. I want her hands to explore my entire body.

"I don't have the truth serum with me." I gasp to catch my breath. Dammit, I really am dizzy, but it's less about the wine now and more about how badly I want Ceri.

When I see the crestfallen change in her expression, I cradle her face in my hands. "But, if you're willing, I can still make you feel that way. I could dominate your mind, if you want it."

Goddess, I'd do anything for her in this moment. As much as

I'd been annoyed by Gina's request to have me dance naked on her balcony, I'd install a pole on Ceri's to spin on it all night for her.

"Please do it." Her body presses against mine, her breasts crushing mine. The way my nipples are so stiff, it sets my body afire for more.

I force myself to step back. I reassure her with a smile that I'm not retreating from her. I need to get my thoughts under enough control to do this. With that in mind, I somewhat foolishly down the rest of my wine.

Ceri waits by her lounge chair. I look out at the river and take in a deep breath. The smell of the gas fire overpowers any other scents that might waft in from the city. I close my eyes as I roll my head around to crack my neck.

I know how my eyes look when I turn back to Ceri. Mine is the gaze of a predator, the thing she craves.

Chapter 7: Customer Service

I strut back to Ceri. Even though she's slightly taller, it's as if she's the one gazing up at me.

Ceri gasps when I grab the back of her head. Then I place the flat of my other hand against her chest, above her heart. The blood is racing through her, making her heart pound against my palm.

There's a reason people say a thought flows. The things we think form rivers of purpose that run through the mind and move the body. A brain isn't that separate from the rest of the organs in the body, though. Everything about a living being contributes to purpose. The mind and the heart both push purpose through a person, and that's why I place my hand in both places. I'm going to build a dam, a weak one to temporarily change how her thoughts flow.

Her eyes hood as my magic flows into her and shifts the tributaries of ideas to converge on one simple belief.

"You will obey me."

The moan that rips out of her is full of desperate submission.

"Yes, I will obey you."

I lightly slap her. "From now on, you will call me Mistress." If she wants to be dominated, then I'm giving her the full ride.

"Mmmm… Yes, Mistress." Her hips rock as she stands there, eager for me to touch her pussy.

Instead, I run a finger down her throat and across the swell of her breasts. "Is this what you wanted? Your mind helplessly fucked to obey me?"

She whimpers as my hand slips inside her her halter and I rub her pert nipple with my fingertip. "Yes, Mistress."

"If I should try to make you do something you wouldn't want to do, you need only say the word 'book.' Do you understand?"

The entire time I deliver the instruction, she groans under the teasing touch of my fingertip rolling her nipple around.

"I understand, Mistress."

"Good. Now, I want to unwrap my gift." I reach behind her neck and untie the knot of fabric keeping her top up. The satin top drops to bunch around her waist and reveal her breasts. I can't help but step back and marvel at how perfect they are. My mouth waters at the thought of sucking on them.

Another knot at the back of her waist keeps the top from falling off her. I change that, and the top crumples to the floor in a small pile of green satin.

I stroll around her like she's a statue to admire from all sides, my hands running over her and enjoying how smooth her skin is to my touch. She hasn't a tan line, and I can't help but wonder if she ever sunbathes in the nude out here.

There's a zipper on the back of the skirt. I grin, because I realize my fantasy of untying that knot at the front was just that. This is how the skirt comes off, but I can trade in one fantasy for another.

"Are you wearing anything under that skirt?"

"Yes, Mistress."

I kiss the back of her shoulder. "Then take it off, but leave the skirt on."

"Yes, Mistress." She reaches into the slit of her skirt and slides down a lacy, green thong. Damn, I should have ordered her to rip it off. Then again, these are lessons we learn the hard way.

"Very good, Ceri. Now, lie down."

"Yes, Mistress."

Even as she sits on the chair and then rests on her back, there's a vacancy in her eyes. I wouldn't have guessed how fucking drenched that would get me. Maybe I hit her a little too hard, but she's got the safe word, just in case.

"Spread your legs for me."

"Yes, Mistress."

She pulls the skirt up just a bit to get her legs wide open, and the skirt spills out to her sides revealing the small patch of shaved auburn hair between her legs.

"Let's get you a little more comfortable." I move behind her and lower the back of the lounge chair to be almost flat.

I unzip the back of my leather miniskirt and slip it off along with my blue thong. I pull off my top next, leaving me there in nothing but my blue wig and black, thigh high boots.

There's no missing the lust in how she gapes at me. Seems she's not that far gone, after all.

"It's good to obey your Mistress, isn't it?"

"Yes, Mistress."

I straddle her waist and reach behind me to stroke her pussy. Her folds are full and wet, coating my fingers in her juices. Her legs spread even wider to let my fingers push deeper inside.

"Do you like that?"

"Yes, Mistress."

I pull out my fingers, and she whimpers in protest, but then she stares in fascination as I dip one of my fingers in my mouth and lick it clean. Damn, she tastes good. I am gonna eat her out later until she's a screaming, sweaty mess creaming herself all over my face.

"Your Mistress deserves to be pleased, too, so put your hands to work."

"Yes, Mistress." Her fingers run along my labia like they've known exactly how to navigate them all of her life. The way she teases my clit, I swoon, and how I don't cum right then and there, I don't know. I'm determined to stave it off a little longer, though.

I grip her left arm by the bicep with my right hand and prompt her to do the same, grabbing my right, upper arm with her left hand.

Once she's got a firm hold on my arm, I lean back to give her other hand better access to my pussy. Then I reach back to run my fingers along the creases of her cunt.

"Are you a good pussy cat for your Mistress?"

Her hips jerk, desperate to get my fingers back inside her. "Yes, Mistress."

I chuckle. "Then meow for your Mistress, pussy cat."

She meows, and when she does, I slap her pussy with my fingers. She shrieks and meows again without me needing to prompt her. I instantly strike her pussy again.

"Good, pussy cat." I groan as her attentions to my love button grow more insistent. I try not to, but I can't help compare it to what the succubus wraith did to me, and Ceri's touch is even better than the wraith's tongue.

"Does my pussy cat want to cum?"

"Yes, Mistress," she says between groans and grunts as she humps against my hand.

"Then you have to make me cum first, and keep saying you're a slave and belong to your Mistress until you we've both cum." Goddess, I'm so damn close, but I want to savor this as long as I can.

My body has other notions, though. All too quickly, I'm humping frantically against her fingers as she keeps declaring her devotion to me.

"I'm a slave and belong to my Mistress." Ceri's eyes roll back in her head as she says the words, and her legs bend up, spreading them wider for me.

"That's right, slave. Keep saying it!"

Fuck, I'm almost there! Her fingers caress my clitoris, gently squeezing and twisting.

"I'm a—I'm a—oh Fuck—I'm a slave! Yes! I belong— Belong!—Belong to my Mistress! Fucking slave! Fucking slave to my Mistress! I belong to you!"

Her hand, wrapped in a death grip around my bicep, burns with friction as she obediently holds me in place with my hold on her upper arm equally tight. My back arches like a bow, lost in the joy of her touch and insane babbles of devotion to me.

"Slave! Slave to my Mistress! Slave! Slave! Slave! SLAVE!"

I scream as the tide drowns me. I almost don't notice the way her own body convulses around my fingers, buried deep inside her.

We still cling to each other so I don't fall back. Hard, fast gasps for air fill the silence between us as our lungs struggle to breathe and our hearts slow their beating.

When my eyes open and I manage to sit up enough to look down at Ceri, the vacancy of enthrallment still paints her eyes.

Oh, we have so much longer to go tonight.

"For the rest of this night, your name is only Slave."

"Yes, my Mistress. My name is Slave."

I dismount her body. How my wobbly legs don't give out, especially in the high heels of my boots, I don't know, but I walk over to my lounge chair and lie down.

"Slave, come here and service my pussy with your tongue."

"Yes, my Mistress!" The eagerness in Ceri's response makes my pussy tingle with renewed yearning.

She stands, and I snap my fingers at her in a warning. "Slaves crawl on their hands and knees. And lose the skirt."

"Yes, my Mistress!" She unzips and pushes the skirt down past her hips to spill to the floor. Then she drops to her knees so fast, I worry for a moment she might hurt herself, but she shows no sign of pain as she crawls naked to the foot of my lounge chair and climbs onto it.

I'm panting again as those empty eyes focus on the place between my legs. She draws closer, like a serpent winding their way towards their prize. The touch of her tongue jolts my pussy, sensitive from their first orgasm of the night. She starts with slow, long licks.

"Yes, Slave," I whisper. I bend my legs until my knees are close to my chest. I reach to hold them wide open, but Ceri recognizes my unspoken wish and obeys. She grabs the insides of my thighs and pushes them up and wide. She purrs as she lavishes attention on me, and the sensation is like a vibrator between my legs, especially as she sucks on my clit.

The orgasm pulls a long moaning "Fuck!" out of me. I haven't told Ceri to stop, though, so she obediently continues. My mind floats on the aftershocks, reduced to nothing but animal cravings for more carnal pleasure. I don't remember grabbing her by her auburn hair, but as the minutes of bliss pass, I realize I'm not giving her a chance to retreat, even if the notion could enter her thoughts. My world is reduced to chasing the peaks her tongue can take me to. When I crest for a third time, a long whimpering moan is the best I can manage. I want her to fuck me all night, and the wicked notion of leaving her like this—a mindless thrall—tempts me for a dangerously long time. I could do it, trap her like this. As desperately as she begged me to do it, making her into my mindless fuck toy for the rest of her life would be oh so easy, and I want her so much. The image of her chained to my bed fixes into my thoughts, and the notion alone is enough to get me eager for her to keep going.

"You—I, no—You can," I struggle to speak as she's still licking me towards a fresh frenzy for a fourth time, "No, stop."

Her tongue abates and her hands release my aching legs, which immediately collapse to hang limp off the sides of the chair.

I gaze on Ceri as she says through her own gasps, "Yes, my Mistress."

Sitting up, I pull her to me in a kiss, tasting my juices on her submissive tongue.

"We're going to your bed, Slave. Bring the wine. I'm going to pour it on you and lick it off."

"Yes, my Mistress."

I chuckle as she attempts to follow my command as she crawls, and as tempting as that might be to play out, it doesn't seem practical.

"You can stand and walk now, Slave."

"Yes, my Mistress."

We don't make it to the bed. Not right away. We stop first at her dining room table, and I eat her out there as she screams more declarations of her devotion to her Mistress.

Fortunately for Ceri's mattress, the wine is long gone by the time we reach her bed, but our need to drink in one another lasts much later into the night.

I wake to a scorcher of a headache and an eyeful of sunshine. When I roll over, I discover Ceri is gone, but the luscious scent of coffee beckons from the kitchen, giving me the incentive to crawl out of the bed.

Where are my clothes? I groan as I remember they're all scattered on Ceri's balcony and the floor next to her dining room table. Even as intimate as we've gotten, I'd prefer not to walk out of the bedroom with nothing on in the harsh daylight.

That's when I spot the neatly folded items resting at the foot of the bed. The blue thong is mine, but the blue t-shirt and black shorts must belong to Ceri. As I dress, I discover my cell phone resting beneath the clothes.

There's a three-word text from Kelly. *'Call me. Now.'* I've also got several "missed call" notifications for her. Shit!

First things first. I walk out of the bedroom and towards the scent of coffee and the sound a knife cutting quickly through what I hope will be some food.

Ceri smiles to me from behind the counter in her kitchen. "Your timing is perfect," she pauses, her grin turning saucy, "my Mistress."

My cheeks warm. I still can't believe I did that last night. My wobbly legs certainly provide added proof of last night's debauchery. I lean against the opposite side of the kitchen island, grateful for the distance between us. As exhausted and sore as I am, my heart quickens with desire for her. She's dressed in a white, v-neck t-shirt that looks like a match for the blue one I'm wearing. Instead of shorts, she's wearing tan pants.

"I made coffee, if you want some," she points with her knife over to the coffee pot. "I can boil some water, if you'd rather have tea."

"No, coffee is good."

"There's some half and half in the refrigerator, if you need it."

I venture behind the counter with Ceri and pour myself some much-needed headache assistance. As I take my first sip, I inspect the items on Ceri's cutting board: black olives and tomatoes. There's also a block of feta cheese awaiting her knife, and cubed potatoes are turning crispy in her air fryer.

"I'll be frying up some eggs, too. I trust you're hungry." Goddess, she's gorgeous and irresistible, the way she smirks at me over her shoulder.

I realize I haven't responded, ensnared by the way her skin glows in the sunlight, when she sets the knife down and turns to face me. She sashays over and pulls me into a kiss. I groan into the embrace. Her body feels perfect against mine, as if I'd been pressed into warm honey. My head throbs and my wearied body screams for rest, but if she slipped her hands beneath my shirt right now, I'd take her to the floor and make love to her again.

She nuzzles her cheek to mine and whispers into my ear. "Thank you for last night."

"Thank you for trusting me."

She pulls back to look me in the eyes. "I do trust you. With all my heart."

Her words fill me with a rush of warmth. I want her, and it's more than lust. I want to keep her close and never let her get away. That I've only known her a few days doesn't matter. It should, though. Love doesn't work like this, does it? The idea that I might be in love, that Ceri has me besotted terrifies me, because what happens when she realizes I can't do anything to the woman who hired her mother's killer? Will she ever forgive that? Does her trust only last as long as I'm investigating this case? I don't think I can handle being cast aside. The way she feels against me is perfection, and I want to do whatever it takes to make this last.

I shriek as my phone rings in the pocket of my borrowed shorts, the vibration startling me more than the loud ringtone of chimes.

As soon as I pull out the phone, I see it's Kelly calling again. "I need to take this. Sorry."

"I'll have breakfast ready by the time you get done."

I stroll out onto the balcony with my coffee as I answer the phone.

"Where the hell have you been?" Kelly yells before I can even say "Hello."

"Sorry, I was sleeping. Was a rough night, but I found the killer I was looking for."

Kelly's tone shifts hard from anger to concern. "You didn't get hurt did you?"

"I'm fine. Just sore." I decide to leave out the soreness has more to do with my sexcapades with Ceri than my encounter with that murderous thief.

"Please tell me you found the crown."

"What?" Ugh... I should have had more coffee before answering her call.

"The laurel crown made of gold." Kelly sounds ready to crawl through the phone for an answer. "Did you find it?"

"No, I found all of the artifacts except that one." I set my coffee mug on the glass table on the balcony and sit on one of the lounge chairs. "The thief was hired to steal those items. She gave the crown to someone else."

"Fuck! You've got to find it."

"Kelly, what's so important about it?"

"I'm certain it's the Crown of Aphrodite."

I rub my forehead. Too much wine and not enough coffee yet. "I've never heard of it."

"Anyone wearing the crown can enthrall and control any woman in their presence."

That makes me sit up.

Kelly keeps going. "Please tell me you know who the thief gave that crown to."

My fun last night was probably a bad idea, because I'm gonna need all of my strength for what's ahead of me.

"Yeah, I know who she gave it to." I sigh. "Anessa Kotov."

There's a long pause on the other end of the phone before Kelly responds.

"The Queen Dragon of the city? That Anessa Kotov?"

"Yes."

"Well, that's terrible."

Chapter 8: Scales of Injustice

I call Anessa Kotov—or rather, her assistant—as soon as I leave Ceri's apartment.

When the assistant puts me on hold, she sounds so annoyed by my call that I'm certain the Queen Dragon of the city will refuse to meet. But the assistant comes back on the line in less than a minute and tells me the time and place. She still sounds pissed with me, though.

While a part of me would prefer to get the meeting over with during the day, having our meet set for nine at night gives me more time for a nap to recover from my bedroom Olympics with Ceri and the confrontation with her mother's killer.

Later that night, I can just make out Ceri's apartment building off to the east as I drive across the 32nd Street Bridge over the Boleyn River to the south side of the city. I wonder if she's watching from her balcony and sees my black car moving along the bridge. My mind keeps going back to Ceri at all the wrong times. As potent as the memory of the night we met was, last night has dwarfed that brief encounter. Even the feel of her body against mine when we kissed this morning before breakfast distracts me the second my mind is given any time to wander.

My phone's GPS directs me west until I'm just short of the county line. My car's engine groans as I take a steep road, up to Anessa Kotov's mansion.

About ten minutes before nine o'clock, I come to a stop as I reach the ten-foot tall, brick wall with an iron gate that surrounds the Queen Dragon's estate. A woman with silver hair pulled into a short ponytail and dressed in a black suit and tie steps out of a guard shack just outside the gates.

She stops several feet away from the car, and it takes a second for me to realize she's keeping herself out of reach of my car door, if I tried to swing it open and hit her with it. After she studies me, she looks into the back seat of my car.

"Your name?" she asks.

"Monica Devlin, I have an appointment."

She points towards the back of my car. "Open the trunk."

"Are you kidding me?"

The way she arches an eyebrow at me makes it clear she's asking just how serious I am about wanting to meet with her boss. For a moment, I wonder if this is the assistant I spoke with this morning, but the voice doesn't match. This one has more of a New York accent. Come to think of it, I couldn't place the accent of the woman I spoke to earlier today.

I reach down with my left hand and pop open the trunk. The guard walks back there for a look, but she never places herself directly behind the car, probably to make sure I don't throw the car in reverse and hit her with my bumper. While she's doing that, she brings her left wrist up to her mouth and talks into what I assume is a radio. "I've got a Monica Devlin here to meet with Ms. Kotov." I can't make out what the person on the other end of the radio says. The guard slams the trunk shut and walks back up to the driver side window, still staying out of reach.

"You're clear to enter. Stay on the main road, no turns. After you park your car, walk straight to the front door, and whatever you do, don't step on the grass." The way she says that last part makes it clear that her boss isn't worried about the lawn maintenance. They probably have some creatures trained to attack anyone who sets foot in the forest surrounding the estate. The guard doesn't elaborate, though. Instead, she disappears back into the guard shack and the iron gate slides open without a shriek of metal.

I know from mapping this address that the mansion sits on a small cliff overlooking the Boleyn River, but the enormity of the white brick mansion hides that view. The driveway in front of the mansion offers dozens of places I might park, because no one else is parked here. I guess Kotov and her staff park in a separate place on the estate.

I pull up my skirt a bit to get out of the car. Given the woman I'm meeting tonight, a t-shirt and jeans won't cut it. I pulled out the only little black dress I own. My mothers got this as a gift for me years ago. I once made the mistake of googling the dress and confirmed how insanely expensive it must have been. This baby has a split v-neckline with a gathered waist and goes down just far enough to cover my knees. I even wore high heels for this, and I almost never do that.

When I climb up to the front door and knock on it, I expect an immediate answer. Instead, I'm left standing here for at least three minutes. Yes, this place is huge, but I'm certain this is supposed to scare me, as if the giant fucking mansion on a cliff and the guard out front weren't intimidating enough.

The door jerks open so fast that I jump. Must have been obvious, because the woman greeting me goes from a scowl to a smirk.

"Let's not keep my Lady waiting."

As soon as she speaks, I know this is the assistant I spoke with on the phone. She's not what I expected. For some reason, I had this idea of someone much taller and muscular, but she looks about my height. I'm only five foot seven. She's dressed in a black jacket over a red turtleneck and black pants. Her blond hair is pulled back into a tight braid that reaches down to her ass. If I wore my hair pulled that tight, I'd have a headache. Maybe it does hurt her head. Might explain her sour disposition.

She turns without waiting for me to respond and leads me deeper into the darkly-lit mansion. Her black dress shoes click against the granite floor with an impatient rhythm. My shoes click even faster, because while we might be the same height, she's more legs than I am.

This place is enormous. The foyer alone is a vast hall with even larger rooms beyond it in all directions. She leads me straight ahead and towards a pair of doors set within a curved wall. The room within must be a large circle, going by the shape of the wall in front of me. As we get closer, I notice what look like white coats hanging on hooks on each side of the doors.

We stop outside the doors, and she pivots to face me. "Take off your clothes and put on the cloak." She points to one of the white cloaks I'd mistaken for coats.

"I don't think so."

She rolls her eyes. "In less than three minutes, you're either going through those doors in what you're wearing now," she points to the doors leading back outside and then switches to the doors in front of us, "or these doors wearing nothing—and I mean nothing—but a smile and that robe. The smile is optional; the rest isn't."

My nostrils flare as I fight the urge to hit this woman. I'd ask where I can change, but I can already guess the answer. I can't believe I got dressed up for this bitch, and now I've got to toss it all to the floor. I reach behind me and pull the zipper down far enough to squeeze out of my dress, I don't let it fall to the floor, though. I was serious about how expensive this dress is, so I pull off the white robe, toss that to the floor and put my dress on the hook in its place. I don't miss the way Anessa's assistant enjoys the show as I slip out of my shoes, bra, and panties. Those I leave on the floor beneath where my dress hangs.

The robe is pure silk, split down the front, that I tie off with a sash. That doesn't do much to preserve any dignity when the robe doesn't even make it down to mid-thigh.

Now that I'm dressed for the occasion, I glare at the assistant with a silent demand to open the doors. She scowls at me again as she speaks. "You'd have been smarter to go out the other doors, but it's your choice."

She pushes open the doors to the round room.

Steam wafts out into the foyer. As soon as I enter the room, the doors shut behind me.

The only light in the room comes from above. A glass dome admits what moonlight there is tonight, but the steam obscures most of it. I can see only a few feet in any direction. The floor is no longer marble. It feels like stone tiles, but I can't see them clearly enough to be certain.

There's a scent to the air in the room, something sweet. The warm, wet steam causes the robe to cling to me, and I break into a sweat.

The room is so hot that it's difficult to breathe. The steam almost scalds my throat and lungs in a way that's uncomfortable and yet strangely pleasant, like a shot of tequila. My skin tingles, a sensation that spreads across my entire body. I gasp as I fight to take a deep breath, because I'm getting dizzy.

"Monica Devlin."

The voice, sultry and commanding, jolts me to attention. There are flames visible ahead, so I walk towards them. The silhouette of a woman appears in the steam. Red eyes, glowing like embers, focus on me.

"You must be Anessa Kotov." Despite my best efforts, I can only speak in a breathy voice. The steam is overpowering.

She doesn't answer. Instead she walks to her right, leans that way a bit and flames erupt from her lips to ignite a small cauldron atop a stone pillar. She turns to her left and does the same.

I stare in fascination, both at the sight of this woman breathing fire from her lips and from the reveal of her beauty in the firelight. I'd expected someone much older, but she could claim to be twenty-five, and I'd believe her. She is tall and slender, but not in a way that suggests she's frail. Her brown hair dances as if caught in the wind, but the air doesn't stir in here. Flames flow through her dark locks, and that must have been what let me see her earlier. The red eyes, though, they betray her age. This one is ancient, far more than the four decades she's held the title of this city's Queen Dragon.

She wears a blood red silk robe, similar to mine, but hers reaches down to the floor and flows behind her like a royal cape. The split reveals far more of her cleavage than I've allowed mine to. Even though her breasts appear small, the way that robe frames her curves is distracting.

"I've been wondering when you would call on me, sorceress." She grins as my eyes widen in surprise.

"Oh, yes," she says. "You're making quite the reputation for yourself. This world has so many vampires, shape-shifters, and all other manner of mystical beings. Some mortals can perform true magic, but there are precious few who can reach a level great enough to claim the title of sorceress."

She stalks around me in a circle, drawing closer. I try to watch her the entire time, but turning in place makes me dizzier. I stumble but manage to stay upright. I muffle a chuckle at my clumsiness, and I instantly realize how out of character that reaction is for me.

"I'm here on business."

She stops off to my left. I blink as I try to focus on her more clearly. The fire in the cauldrons helps, despite the steam filling the room.

"You surprise me." She tilts her head to the side, studying me intently. "I know you found my thief and tricked her into confessing to murdering a woman and so much more, and yet she told them nothing about me. Why is that?"

"I was protecting my client." Saying that is a struggle, but I can tell my mind is starting to clear a bit. With my focus returning, I realize the steam is also thinning, and I suspect that isn't a coincidence.

"No, no, no." Anessa says that as if scolding a child caught reaching into the proverbial cookie jar. She cups her palm in front of her face, using it as a funnel as she blows out a long stream of smoke. No, not smoke. As it engulfs me, I realize this is the steam that's filling the room.

This isn't an elaborate steam room. The Queen Dragon has filled it with her own breath. I try not to inhale the steam, but she's caught me off-guard, too late to swallow any clean air. The fresh influx of warm vapor hits my brain almost instantly, and a pleasant vertigo drops me to my knees. The landing hurts my legs, but the pain is drowned by my intoxication.

I giggle again as I stay on the floor, on my knees. When I manage to look up, I find Anessa staring down at me.

My Goddess... She's even more beautiful up close. Her skin is flawless and pale.

"I'm told you only work for women. Is that true?"

She strokes my face with the back of her fingers, the tips of her pointed fingernails lightly grazing my cheeks without drawing blood. I moan and lean into her touch. "Yes," I whisper back. "Only women."

"Then perhaps one day, you'll be willing to work for me."

Thinking is so hard, and the effort delays my reply. When I do answer, the best I manage is a slurred "No."

Anessa smiles down at me, and in spite of myself, I smile back.

"Tell me what you want, little sorceress. What brought you here tonight?"

"The crown. Belongs to my client." The words slur out of me, and then I fall silent, save for another moan as she runs her thumb over my lips.

"Oh, that is a pity. You see, I don't have the crown. That bauble is for controlling women, and as you're no doubt noticing, I hardly need help in doing that, do I?"

I'm too busy licking the tip of her thumb and her sharp fingernail to answer, proving her point.

"Tell me, you sweet thing." She leans down and with her hand that I'm not busy licking like a horny cat, she hooks a finger through the sash of my robe and pulls loose the knot. "What will you give me if I tell you who I gave the crown to?"

I grunt as I thrust out my chest, arching my back, eager to free my breasts from the robe for her. I know she wants them, and I want her to touch them.

Wait… No. I can't do this. I need to stop. Need to…

But then she's running her sharp fingernails over my chest, sliding the robe out of the way. The steam caresses my bare breasts. I luxuriate in the sensation, eyes rolling back in my head as she then pinches the pert and eager nipple on my right breast.

"Now, now, sorceress, tell your Queen what you'll give her for the information on who took the crown?" She grins as she plucks her fingers from between my lips, and I whimper.

"Don't. Know." I gaze up into those red eyes that hold my complete attention. "Can't. Think."

Her smile widens, and her teeth are sharp like a shark's. The sight of them doesn't startle or frighten me. I simply gaze in fascination.

"Then I shall think for you." Anessa's voice fills the room and all the empty space in my mind.

"Think," I whisper as she lowers me onto my back. "Think. For me."

She brings one of those long, slender fingertips to her lips and shushes me. "You needn't speak, my pet." She reaches between my legs and one of those razor-sharp nails traces a path around my pussy but without ever directly touching it. The sensation of pleasure offered and denied makes me swoon. I arch my back, trying to guide her hand to slip inside, but I'm too clumsy to make it happen. I whimper as I collapse flat onto my back again.

When she next speaks, I realize her lips aren't moving. *"You can answer me just fine without speaking aloud, and I have better things for your lips to do."* Her voice echoes within my mind, and as I stare in fascination, she reaches for the sash of her robe and shrugs it off, collapsing into a pile of red silk on the floor.

With the robe removed, a pair of black, leathery wings stretch out behind her, as if she might take flight. Instead, Anessa saunters over to just beside my head. The tip of a slender, forked tongue slips out to lick her lips, and my heart races in anticipation. A long strand of her brown hair runs down the middle of her chest and over left breast. When she pushes the hair back over her pale shoulder, her hair alights so that it appears as if her crowning glory is nothing but fire itself. Her red eyes glow.

She steps over me, so that her feet are on each side of my head. Her pussy glistens in the faint firelight.

"Let's negotiate what all you will do for me to get the information you desire," she thinks into my mind.

"Yes." I hiss out the word as my gaze pulls away from her face to look between her legs, because something is moving behind her, and I realize it's a long tail, covered in dark red scales ending in a point. The tail twists like a snake, as if anticipating on where it might strike. Its movements are hypnotic.

"Would you like to honor your Queen?" she thinks into my mind, and it crashes over my other thoughts, pulling my gaze back to meet hers. *"Would you enjoy worshiping your Queen?"* she asks as she lowers herself, bringing her pussy to my lips.

My tongue answers for me, running over the edges of her pussy lips. She tastes like cinnamon, and I growl as I savor her.

My kisses pull a gentle laughter out of her as her thoughts fill my mind. She strokes my hair like I'm a pet who belongs to her, and the thought of the comparison makes me so horny.

"Would you like to know what you will give your Queen for this

information you seek?"

One word fills my thoughts as I continue to eagerly lick her cunt. *"Yes!"*

This time, she speaks aloud. "You will give me everything."

My breath catches and the ministrations of my tongue stutter as something silky brushes against the insides of my thighs.

"Your mind." She thinks to me as the tip of her tail strokes my pussy. *"Your soul. And every luscious bit of your body."*

I shriek as the pointed tip of her tail slips inside me, filling me. I hump on her tail with eager abandon. I've enjoyed my share of dildos and strap-ons, but they are nothing compared to the sensation of her silky scales gliding in and out of me.

"Keep licking, my sweet sorceress." These words she speaks aloud, and as I look up at her, I see the curl of her lips, her wicked amusement at my predicament.

I lick at her with greater abandon, but a thought tickles the back of my mind. There's this notion of wrongness to all this, but I can't remember why I should resist this as I glide my tongue around her spicy cunny.

"Are your ready to surrender to your Queen?"

Her red eyes blaze, flames dancing within them.

"Surrender?" I think, struggling to remember why I shouldn't, knowing somehow it would be wrong.

"If you want to know who has the crown, you must give yourself to me." She purrs as I continue to please her, my body writhing beneath her.

My ass slaps against the stone floor as I struggle to cum on her tail, but somehow, I can't. It's as if she knows exactly how much pleasure to give me without pushing me over that blessed precipice.

She chuckles. *"Oh, you are so desperate for it."*

"Yes!"

"No, no, no... When you address me, you shall address me as your Queen." The words aren't any louder than the previous ones in my thoughts, but somehow, these carry a weight that crushes all of my other thoughts.

I know she expects my reply, and the words given thought bring me even closer to the orgasm I need. *"Yes, my Queen!"*

My words please her, causing her to take in a sharp breath and then let out a long stream of flames into the air above us.

Something wordless fills my thoughts, and it's her own pleasure, a thought so strong that it's shared into my mind through this profane connection. I want more. If I please her more, I know my body will find the peak it craves.

"Then give all of yourself to your Queen, and I will tell you who took the crown."

The offer makes my thoughts stumble, because the mention of the crown conjures the memory of Ceri.

"No!" my Queen says as she grips my hair tight forcing my gaze to stay on hers. She puckers her lips and then blows out a long blast of steam into my face. The instant rush of that delightful narcotic numbs my mind, and my world focuses only onto pleasure: fucking her tail and licking her cunt. *"Surrender to your Queen!"*

As badly as I want to cum, as much as I feel this insane need to please my Queen, the thought of Ceri fights it. A part of me hates how much thinking of Ceri is keeping me from cumming, but I also feel that purpose that drove me here.

"Can't!"

My Queen slaps me with the back of her hand. "How dare you refuse your Queen!"

The sharp pain focuses my mind just a bit. "Please! I need it!"

My mind feels like it will shatter if I don't cum.

"Then surrender all that you are! Vow your service to me!"

I want to tell her I will, but her face contorts in confusion. She can sense I won't break, no matter how much my body wants me to.

"A favor then," she says, her voice a hiss of fascination and rage. "You will pay me a favor for anything I demand."

I take a long lick of her cunt. This time, the attempt to please her is deliberate, a manipulation, because I know she's enjoying it. The pleasure is enough to even distract her strong mind.

"I won't kill anyone for you, won't hurt them."

Issuing the conditions takes all of what little self control I have left. She chuckles as she pulls my face up into her pussy, her legs spreading wider to give me even greater access to pleasure her. I try to think of any other conditions I should demand, but I'm too close to that orgasm that she's strategically denied and held so cruelly close.

"No." She laughs as she rides on my face, blasting more flames into the air. *"Hurt is too vague, but I'll agree to no physical harm."*

"Yes, please! Please!"

She purrs. *"Then let us seal our pact."* She screams in delight. *"Together."*

We linger in that moment, her tail manipulating me like a toy for her to fuck into sweet submission, striking that spot that hungers for her touch. When we cum at the same time, she cries out in a monstrous, inhuman shriek. Her cinnamon sweet juices spill down my throat as she cums on my face.

Once the moment has passed, she writhes in place above me with a pleased groan. "You will repay this favor, my sweet sorceress."

When Anessa stands, she strolls over to the burning cauldrons and looks over her shoulder and the top edge of her wing at me.

"I was paid by an anonymous customer to retrieve the crown and give it to a man named Jonathan Baxter. I'll have my other servant give you their address."

I'm too exhausted to do anything but breathe and watch her in fascination as she reaches into the air and clenches a fist. Her hand motion snuffs out both cauldrons, causing her to vanish into the mist.

Her footsteps echo into the distance until she's gone, leaving me there in a pathetic heap on her floor.

Her "other servant."

Fuck. I agreed to only one favor, but that's enough for her to consider me her property. As I struggle to find enough strength to even consider the act of standing, I realize she's right. I've just made a deal with a monster. But that's a problem for another day.

For now, I have the information I need and no time to waste. I've got to find Johnathan Baxter before he can deliver the crown to the person responsible for all of this.

Chapter 9: Burned Bridges

Leaving the steam room (that isn't a steam room) is a unique "walk of shame." The servant with the long blonde braid silently watches me get back into my dress with this knowing look that seems one part sympathy and two parts disgust. Hard to say how much of that is just how I'm seeing myself. A part of me knows I shouldn't feel that way. My Queen—Dammit!—Anessa got the drop on me. No denying that, but I managed to avoid her turning me completely to her service. There's going to be a day I pay for this, but that's just how it goes sometimes. Bridges to cross and all that.

Before I leave, the assistant hands me a sheet of paper with Jonathan Baxter's name and address on it. I'm tempted to go straight to his place, but I'm not dressed for it. Instead, I drive home to change into a t-shirt and jeans. After I slip on a denim jacket, I stop by my safe and pull out my ring. Enchanted objects are a real thing, and they can enhance a sorceress's power, but they always come at a price. I decide this might be a night to take that risk and slide the silver band onto my right index finger.

The address is south of the river, just inside the suburbs. I've lived downtown for so many years now that it's always mind-boggling to me how dark it gets once I leave the city limits. It's like driving through air made of tar with the random street light offering the bare minimum of illumination to let you see where I'm going without showing me anything of the actual surroundings.

As if the dark wasn't enough to make me uncomfortable, the condition of the houses is. Most of them look twice my age and barely bigger than my apartment. I park on the road a couple houses down from Jonathan Baxter's address. His front yard, illuminated by a single light post in the middle of it, is disturbingly pristine. The grass is so neatly trimmed and vibrant, he could rent it out as a putting green. A pickup truck that's absurdly big and screams "compensating" eats up most of his driveway. I walk up the paved drive on the far side of the pickup to hide myself from view, just in case he looks out his window. I feel the hood of the truck, and it's cold.

I don't see any lights on inside the house, so maybe he went to bed early. It's only about 10:30. Then again, maybe these suburb types consider that late.

My thumb rubs against the ring on my finger, as if that might warm it up to do its thing. After all, if I do wake this guy from a stone-cold sleep, I get the feeling he's the type to answer the door with a gun in his hand.

I plan to knock on his front door like a police officer ready to make an arrest, but then I see the door isn't shut.

The realization comes just five feet from the door and stops me in my tracks. I've heard of people outside the city being comfortable leaving their doors unlocked, but something tells me Jonathan Baxter isn't the type to take that so far as to leave his front door sitting wide open for anyone to waltz inside.

Staying still, I don't hear anything but the crickets and my breathing. I stay there long enough for a car to crawl its way down the street and keep going.

I can't stand here all night, but I'm not eager to stroll into a stranger's house like this. Thinking the incantation to heighten my soul's sight, I study the house. What I see catches me unprepared. The house is aflame with mystical energy. It's as if someone set off the magical equivalent of a pipe bomb inside this place. I don't sense any life in there, but I'm not sure I could with all the magical "white noise" obscuring my soul sight.

Fuck it.

I walk up to the door and bang on the frame as hard as I can, which hurts my knuckles.

"Mr. Baxter?" I call into the house but don't shout. Last thing I want is to draw out any neighbors. Although, these houses have a lot of space between them with trees providing added privacy, so there's a good chance of no one hearing or seeing me.

No one answers, and there's still no sound of anyone moving in there. On the bright side, that means I'm not likely to meet anyone with a gun in their hand. On the downside, I still have no clue what's going on here.

That all changes as soon as I see Jonathan Baxter in the middle of his wood-paneled living room.

He's on his knees, with his arms positioned as if to grab at his temples, but his forearms end in broken stubs. His face is frozen in a mask of pain, jaw wide enough to suggest he met his end screaming. There's no blood. His entire body is charred to the point that he's more like a statue of ash. The missing hands are on the floor, too far away from the rest of his body to have simply fallen off. Someone tossed them aside.

All I can think is that this fool tried to use the Crown of Aphrodite. The magic fried him. Was it because he's a man? Possible, but perhaps it was because he lacked any innate magical ability. A glance at this house doesn't show any outward sign of mystical talents. He has a deer head mounted on his wall, along with several shot guns and bows and arrows. He doesn't strike me as anything other than a guy who had a weak ego and liked to pick on animals.

The idea that it's because he's a man seems to fit, though. If a woman wanted someone to deliver the crown, it wouldn't make sense for her to entrust it to a woman who might use it on her instead.

Just as I'm about to consider looking for his cell phone, I spot it on the floor. It's smashed to bits. I don't mean someone stomped on it. I mean someone pulverized it. Most of the protective cell phone case survived, but whatever crushed down on the center of the phone left an inch-wide circle that went through the carpet and into the wooden floor beneath.

I curse under my breath, because this is it. I've hit the end of the path, because whoever ripped off his hands probably did that to pull the crown off his head. They have it, and I've no way to know who they are.

Chapter 10: An Unexpected Guest

There's no debate in my thoughts when I reach the parking garage at my apartment complex. I don't dare call Ceri to tell her what's happened. Suppose part of me knew this would happen, because I hadn't let her know I was meeting with the Queen Dragon tonight.

I live in what used to be the warehouse district, and my building is a converted tobacco warehouse, unlike most of the cookie-cutter buildings that have sprung up around it. As I cross the street from the parking garage to my building, I see someone walking down the sidewalk towards me. The way they move catches my attention.

They walk with purpose, not someone out for a stroll or simply going home, like I am.

I stop with my hand on the glass double doors as I realize who it is.

"Ceri?"

She smiles as I say her name. She's wearing a hunter green, single-shoulder dress that goes just past her knees and a pair of black stiletto high heels. The thin, buckled strap of her leather purse rests on her left shoulder with the strap of the dress.

"I'm sorry." She pulls me into a kiss that I melt into. Perhaps it's the heels, but I hadn't realized just how much taller she is than me. "I couldn't wait to see you again," she whispers as she traces kisses up and down my neck.

I moan as the path of her lips awakens all my lust. The encounter with Anessa left me feeling dirty and cast aside. Being with Ceri washes it away. I cling to her as if to let go might send me tumbling down a cliff. I breathe in the woodsy scent of her hair and whisper her name in her ear.

A twinge of guilt for how I've failed her tonight offers the weakest of protests as I fumble to open the door to the building. We race down the stairs to the sublevel, where my apartment is and crash against the door as we kiss and tug at one another's clothes. I don't know how I get the door to my apartment on, but as soon as we get inside, Ceri strips off my denim jacket and tugs my t-shirt up over my head, producing an audible rip in the cotton fabric. She's never been this dominant in our previous encounters, but I don't resist it. The feel of her skin against mine is warm and a blessing that makes my whole body tingle with joy.

She chases me into my bedroom where she shoves me back onto my bed. Her eyes blaze with a wicked delight in the sliver of moonlight that pours down through the room's only narrow, flat window.

Her dress is already gone. The way she stands over me in nothing but a brown bra and matching panties makes her look so powerful. I want her to take me, own me. My pussy gushes at the thought of her fingers working their own kind of magic on me.

She jerks my shoes off, tossing them to the floor. I squeal when she rips off my jeans, taking my panties off in the same move, baring nothing but my body for her to take.

Grabbing me by the ankles, she pulls me towards her. I groan, more desperate than ever for her to work her way up to the rest of my body, my pussy lips full and glistening in invitation.

Then she releases her grip on my legs and steps back. I whimper my desperation for her to take me.

Ceri brings a finger to her lips and shushes me with a wicked grin. "I've brought something special for tonight." She struts back into the living room where her dress and purse were tossed to the floor. My stomach drops in awe of the view of her back as her hips sway, until she disappears around the corner of the door.

I realize I'm still wearing my ring, and slip it off, placing it on my bedside table. I'm no novice, so I doubt I'd accidentally burn down the building, but magical weapons are always best left out of sex.

I jump as something vibrates beneath my ass. My phone was in my back pocket and must have come out when Ceri yanked my jeans off. I go to mute the notifications and toss it aside, but then I see the message from Kelly.

'I just read Hannah Tennison's obituary. She doesn't have a daughter!'

Everything in me turns cold. Ceri isn't Hannah's daughter. She's been lying to me this whole time.

"Are you ready?" Ceri stands in the doorway to my bedroom, hand reaching towards the top of the door frame. She's discarded her bra and panties, standing there only in her black, high heels. The sight of her is distracting enough, but as she sashays towards me, the moonlight glints against something metal in her auburn hair. She's wearing a golden, laurel crown.

A wicked smile curls her lips as she steps up to the foot of the bed. I should do something, roll away, cast a spell to fling her back, but my thoughts empty out. A warm sensation unlike anything I've ever experienced fills my chest. My nipples harden and ache for attention.

"That's a good girl." She leans down and strokes her fingertips up the inside of my leg. The cell phone drops out of my hand onto the bed.

Ceri leans over, drawing my eyes to her breasts as she retrieves my phone. She chuckles as she reads Kelly's text and then drops the phone to clatter on the hardwood floor.

"Well, that's unfortunate," Ceri says as she grabs my leg and roughly pulls me towards her. "Not that it matters now. Tell me who you love?"

I answer in a breathy voice. "You." I gaze at her, paralyzed by the desire I feel for her, the overwhelming need that demands I move, to make love to her, but unable to consider acting without her say so. "I love you, Ceri!"

She purses her lips, blowing me a kiss. "I know you do, but I have a confession."

My eyes roll back in my head as she runs her fingers through the trimmed bush of brown hair between my legs.

"You see, I'm not Ceri." When I look back at her, tight curls form in her auburn hair. Her jawline narrows, and those cerulean eyes turn yellow like a wolf's. "Don't worry. We'll be inviting 'Ceri' over to join us soon. You'd like that, wouldn't you?"

"Yes!" I shout it and joy fills my heart as I see her wicked smile widen at my eagerness to do what she wants.

"Oh, this works so well." She taps at the crown in her now

curly hair. "Just one look and you're now my little bitch in heat, aren't you?"

"Yes. Yes! I'll do anything you want!" I'm breathing so hard that I swoon from the effort to speak. Oh, I want her to touch me more. I squirm on the bed, whimpering from the overwhelming need to have her play with my body as much as she's toying with my mind.

This feels like some mythic combination of honey and chocolate mixed with every conceivable depravity. I can't wait for her to tell me how to make her happy and please her.

"My name, you pathetic little mortal, is Artemis, but for the rest of your short existence, you'll call me only Goddess."

"Yes, Goddess!"

She steps away and I whine, humping at the air in my desperation.

"Get on your knees, mortal. Bow before your Goddess."

"Yes, Goddess!" I scramble off the bed now that I have her permission to move and drop to my knees at her feet. I lick my lips, but I'd rather lick her shoes. "Please let me worship you."

"Oh, you shall, and we'll have 'Ceri' join you as my eager acolyte."

"Yes, Goddess!"

The idea of me and Ceri both naked on our knees before Goddess almost makes me cum. My thighs are already slick from my excitement. I imagine Ceri kissing Goddess's left foot as I worship the right. We'd make excellent servants, the best of any who serve Goddess.

"We'll have her join us soon, mortal, once we're prepared. I know that will make you so happy."

There's only one answer, and my response is immediate. "Yes, Goddess!"

She laughs as she reaches down to grab my hair and pulls my face up to her perfect delta, and my response to this is immediate. My tongue worships Goddess.

I spend the entire night worshiping her. Her appetite for pleasure is as great as her beauty. When she finally decides to sleep, she takes the bed, and I lay on the floor at the foot of the bed, ready for her to command me.

In the morning, she lets me back on the bed and massages my cunt with her fingers. She teases me with the promise of slipping them inside as she asks me questions about Ceri, mostly having me tell her about my first meeting with Ceri and my investigation. I let Goddess know how Kelly figured out what the crown is.

After what feels like an hour of questions, Goddess asks, "Has she demonstrated any powers?"

"No, Goddess. She's just a mortal woman."

A single fingertip slides up and down my slit. I shriek with pleasure, but my devotion to Goddess keeps me from moving to force her fingers inside me.

"Are you certain?"

"Yes, Goddess. I was able to use my magic on her mind to make her obey me." I cry out as she dips her finger into me. My hips shudder, feeling how close I am to cumming for her, but I mustn't. She's told me not to. Once I've told her all she wishes to know, she'll let me climax.

"My sister always has been so foolish." She leans down to bring her face within inches of mine. Her yellow eyes, almost as golden as the crown in her auburn hair, hold me enthralled as if some ethereal threads from them have captured my gaze and refuse to release their hold on me, not that I would ever want them to. "For what it's worth, you eager slut, she didn't really lie to you. She has no idea who she really is. We won't be changing that. No, we're going to bring her to her knees beside you, where she belongs. Aren't you excited to help her belong to your Goddess?"

"Yes, Goddess! She'll worship you just as I do." A second finger pushes into me. Mmmmm… This is bliss. "I'll bring her to you! Oh, Goddess! Yes! I'll make her yours! We'll be together at your feet. Worship you! Worship you! Worship you!" A third finger joins the first two and I'm a babbling mess screaming my devotion to Goddess, begging for her to let me cum, because I don't dare do it without her command.

My heart pounds hard enough to make my chest hurt, but I don't let up. I scream my obedience as I ride her divine hand.

"Please! Goddess! Please! Please!!!"

She leans closer and whispers two words into my ear, the two most wonderful words.

"Now, slut."

I scream as my pussy erupts in a fiery surge of delight. My body convulses as her thumb slides along my clitoris.

I gasp for breath, whispering my undying gratitude. I belong to Goddess, and as she tells me her plans for enthralling Ceri, I soak in every word. Ceri will join me, and we'll worship Goddess together forever.

Chapter 11: Sibling Rivalry

I take a long shower and then get myself dressed to capture Ceri for Goddess Artemis. She's told me exactly what to wear.

"She's always been quite the whore," Goddess says, lounging on my bed as I put on the dress she's brought for me. "She won't be able to resist you in that."

The vibrant orange silk feels wonderful as it glides against my nipples. The top of the dress ties behind my neck with two narrow strips of silk running down my chest to barely cover my breasts and form a plunging neckline that stops just short of my crotch, just low enough to make it obvious I'm not wearing any underwear, not that the short skirt with slits going up to my waist on each side make it difficult to tell that already.

It's after sunset when I call Ceri and ask her to come to my apartment.

The time spent waiting for her to arrive is filled with me performing a seduction spell similar to the one I used on the thief. Goddess makes it clear I'm not meant to use it to manipulate her mind. Ceri will belong to Goddess, and then we'll be together.

I down a glass of chilled Riesling and dark chocolate as I initiate the spell, tailoring it to Ceri.

I place my hand over my heart to steady myself as soon as Ceri texts me that she's arrived. Punching a code into my phone unlocks the doors to the building long enough for her to enter.

When I open the door to my apartment, I can't hold in my smile. I'm so excited she's here. We're going to be together, worshiping Goddess. Ceri looks beautiful, even dressed the most casual I've seen her yet. She's wearing the purple jacket she had with her the first night we met, but this time she's wearing it over a black, scoop neck top with blue jeans that cling tightly to the curves of her hips and thighs.

Her eyes widen at she takes in my outfit. "Monica?"

I reach for her hand, twining my fingers into hers and gently pull her inside. "I wanted to surprise you."

Now that she's inside, I flip off the overhead light in my living room. We aren't left entirely in darkness, though. I've dozens of red, black, and white candles lit on the black granite, kitchen counter and around the living room. Her gaze stays on me, though.

I lean in and whisper, "I've poured you a drink."

Her brows furrow, but that doesn't stop her from following me deeper into my apartment. I scoop up one of the glasses of Riesling I poured as soon as she texted me she was here.

She grins at me as I raise my glass in a silent toast. There's a question in her eyes that she hesitates to voice.

I clink our glasses together. "I thought we should celebrate."

"Celebrate?" She shakes her head, but then her eyes widen and she grabs me by the arm. "You found it?"

I nod. "I'll have it here for you soon." And then we'll be

together with Goddess.

I sip my wine, the fruity scent of the Riesling briefly over-powering the smell of melting wax that fills my apartment.

"I want to make you happy again tonight." I take a deep drink of the wine and then set my glass down next to the candles and walk to the center of my small living room. I've pushed the coffee table to the wall beneath the narrow, horizontal windows which are covered by black curtains.

I look over my shoulder and grin. The dress leaves my back bared to her with the top of the skirt starting just past the top of my ass.

The way her blue eyes almost glaze as she admires my body gives me a thrill. The seduction spell is taking hold. Even if she realizes what I'm doing, Goddess thinks she'll trust I'd never take advantage of her, and despite the twinge of guilt I feel in deceiving her, I know Ceri will thank me once we both belong to Goddess.

"You can bring the wine, if you like," I say as I reach up behind my neck and unclasp the top of my dress. The silk spills down to the blankets I've spread out on the floor.

Ceri stares dumbstruck. I can already tell she likes what she sees, even without the seduction spell to pull her in. Even so, I'm worried I've moved too quickly for her, so I stroll back.

I slip my hand around the back of her neck and then pull myself in the rest of the way. Our bodies, hers still dressed and mine naked, come together. I take the half-empty glass of Riesling out of her hand and down it before setting it back on the kitchen counter with a soft clink behind her.

Her arms slip around my body as I lean in to kiss. I want her, and the way she matches the aggression of my kiss makes it clear she yearns just as deeply for me. Even if she'd had any doubts as to what's happening here, the lust brought on by my spell has her hopelessly hooked.

I explore her mouth, more desperate to drink her in than any wine. When I break from the kiss, she doesn't resist as I take her hands into mine and pull her towards the blankets.

She offers no protest as I pull off her purple jacket and drop it the floor. We struggle to strip her, because we're also entangled in the madness of lust. Goddess ordered me to make sure that once we're on the floor to position Ceri with the bedroom door behind her, and following that command proves more difficult than I'd expected. My hunger to make love to Ceri overwhelms me, making it difficult to think of anything other than making love to Ceri.

I don't fail Goddess, though.

I work my way down Ceri's body, tweaking her nipples with my teeth and then my fingers once I've found my way between her legs. I feast on her, and as I build Ceri into a frenzy, she whispers my name in a breathless desperation. I reach between my own legs, slipping my fingers inside myself. My tongue licks her in slow, steady strokes. When she shrieks, I don't let up, sensing how close she is to reaching her climax.

Then her body convulses against my mouth, and I taste her joy gushing out of her. Even though I know it's coming, I'm so caught up in Ceri's body writhing, her thighs almost crushing the sides of my head, that I barely notice Goddess walking out of the shadows of my bedroom to stand over Ceri.

"Hello, Ceri." Goddess's voice echoes with power, even as she adds a mocking lilt to my lover's name. "You now belong to me."

Ceri tenses at the unexpected voice but she goes still before she can try to get up or even speak. Her body relaxes on the floor as the crown enthralls her to Goddess as deeply as it has me. I'm still fingering myself as I watch the words sink into Ceri's mind. Her eyes widen in fascination at our Goddess.

She wears a royal blue toga with a sash going over her left shoulder with the skirt split all the way up to the front of her right leg. Just watching her smile at the sight of Ceri too dumbstruck to even move has me close to cumming.

My grunts draw the attention of Goddess. She arches an amused eyebrow and chuckles. "You've done well, slut. You may cum."

I scream "Yes, Goddess!" as my body obediently climaxes for her. I slump onto my side, giddy from the rush, and then moan as I struggle to recover.

Goddess isn't interested in me now, though. She kneels down over Ceri and grabs her by the hair. "Who owns you, you filthy bitch?"

Ceri doesn't answer. Fear stabs into me and pulls me back up onto my knees. Confusion twists the features of Ceri's angelic face.

No! If she resists, we won't be together, and I need her.

Goddess's expression contorts in rage. She snarls as she yanks hard on Ceri's hair.

"Who owns you?" she shouts. The crown in her hair glows, and the air around it warps like heat from the baked plane of a desert.

Ceri's breathing quickens. Her body doesn't move, except for the heaving of her chest.

"No, no, no," Goddess whispers. Her eyes dart to me. "Perhaps, dear sister, you need more incentive. Get over here, slut. Make her cum again."

I crawl over to Ceri's side and reach between her legs to stroke her labia. I draw slow steady paths along her warm, wet folds.

"We'll be together, Ceri," I whisper as I kiss the hollow of her throat. "Just surrender to Goddess, and she'll let us be together forever."

Ceri takes in a sharp breath. Her eyes roll back in her head.

"Oh, she does want that." Goddess chuckles as she stroke's Ceri's hair. "You want this slut that badly? Well, she's mine now."

"All yours, Goddess," I parrot as I slip my fingers into Ceri, her body primed again for my touch. My teeth tease her nipple, savoring the taste of that hardened tip against my tongue. I direct the power of my seduction spell into my tongue and fingers, heightening the pleasure I give her.

Ceri shivers with delight under my eager ministrations.

"That's it, sister," Goddess says. "All it takes is surrendering to me."

Ceri whimpers as I nibble at her breast. "Surrender," she gasps the word uncertainly.

"That's right." Goddess growls. "Surrender to me, the true Goddess."

"True," she grunts and then whimpers as her hips lift to grind on my insistent hand, "Goddess."

Goddess leans down to bring her eyes inches from Ceri's "Do you want this slut I've made my obedient slave?"

"Yes!"

I feel how close, how eager Ceri is now.

"No, no... Say it right, slut. 'Yes, Goddess'."

Ceri gasps. I look up from where I nibble and lick her nipple to see her wide-eyed desperation. Her mouth works, struggling to form the words as her resistance crumbles.

The crown is as blinding as the sun atop Goddess's head. "Say it!"

Ceri's back arches up, shoving her perfect breast against my mouth as she cums again, and she cries out. "Yes, Goddess!"

Goddess laughs and claps slowly. "Very good. Surrender to me. Say it!"

Ceri stares up in vacant adoration. "I surrender to you, Goddess." She answers with a monotone voice that holds the strangest hint of joy to it. I hadn't thought it possible for someone to speak with those two qualities to their words, even after how I manipulated her mind for her the other night.

"Stop, slut. You've done your job."

"Yes, Goddess." I pull away from Ceri's warm body and sit up on my knees to gaze up at Goddess in adoration. The golden, laurel crown no longer burns, having finished its work upon my lover's mind. Now that Goddess has claimed her, Ceri and I can be together.

Goddess grabs Ceri's hair again and yanks hard. "Who do you belong to?"

Ceri's vacant expression and faint smile don't alter at all, despite the rough handling of her body.

"I belong to you, Goddess."

Goddess laughs.

"You're just a mindless slut, aren't you?"

"Yes, Goddess."

"Say it!"

Ceri answers without a second's hesitation. "I'm just a mindless slut, Goddess."

"Say you're fucking trash!"

"I'm fucking trash, Goddess."

Goddess unleashes a sharp laugh and then slaps Ceri across the face.

Chapter 11: Sibling Rivalry

"You deserve to be treated like the filth you are, don't you?"

"Yes, Goddess. I deserve to be treated like filth."

Goddess slaps her again, and she doesn't pull the force of it. Ceri's head snaps hard to the side before rolling back to blankly stare up at Goddess. The sound of that strike echoes in my heart, and a feeling of panic chills my insides.

I want us to be together. Goddess will let us be together. She said we would.

Goddess yanks on Ceri's hair again with a cruel twist of her lips. She looks over at me and grins. "Would you like to know who this slut really is?"

My body shakes, but despite my uncertainty, I know the answer Goddess wants and expects. "Yes, Goddess."

"This is my dear sister," she says in a mocking voice as she slaps Ceri's face. "This is Aphrodite. My dear father's favorite, but you're worthless, aren't you?"

Ceri answers in that mindless tone. "Yes, Goddess. I'm worthless."

No, this isn't what was supposed to happen.

"You always were foolish, sister. When I sent these mortals after your crown, I was only hoping to have a bit of fun at your expense, but then I found out what you'd done to get it back."

Goddess grins at me. "I'll wager she suspected you'd be too suspicious of working for a goddess, even one as substandard as she is. So she made herself into this mortal form, convincing herself of the lie she needed to tell you to work for her."

She slaps Ceri twice, back and forth. "That was a mistake, you fucking slut. Say you're a worthless fool!"

"I'm a worthless," she stumbles in her response as our Goddess slaps her again, "fool, Goddess."

The urge to tell Goddess to stop chokes me. I can't do that. I can't argue with Goddess! I'm her slave!

All I manage is to whimper.

"Did you think I'd forgotten how you seduced my servants all those many centuries ago?" Another slap. "Well, now I'm going to make that little slut you love so much fuck me in front of you, and then I'll order her to beat you with a stick."

No.

Something in me breaks. I have to obey Goddess, but I need Ceri. I love her!

"Kiss me, slut. Kiss your Goddess."

I do as I'm commanded. "Yes, Goddess."

I lean over to Goddess and grab the back of her neck as I pull her into a kiss. I pour all my passion into the embrace. For a moment, I swoon and almost lose myself in the moment. Goddess is so beautiful and perfect, but I love Ceri.

My hands move up her neck and then I reach up to snatch the crown from her and shove it onto Ceri's head.

Artemis screams in rage as Ceri's eyes and the crown flare a brilliant golden light. I'm shoved up off the ground as Artemis grasps me by the throat and lifts me, but she realizes the mistake too late. She should have gone for the crown.

Ceri grabs her by the front of her dress. Artemis drops me to redirect her attention to Ceri, but she's too slow to save herself from being flung against the coffee table and the wall. Artemis cracks against the bricks, shattering them.

Nothing in Ceri's appearance changes as she stands. Even as I'm gasping to recover from Artemis choking me, I stare in awe at the power emanating from the stranger standing in the middle of my apartment. Regal and powerful don't begin to describe her. That she's naked only makes her appear that much more intimidating.

"How. Dare. You!" Ceri doesn't move on her sister but the air between them is abuzz with mystical energy. "You murdered Hannah, my crown's protector! And what you did to her is equally vile!" Her glare stays fixed on Artemis as she points at me.

Artemis stumbles onto her feet. My wall looks worse than she does, but she's still not steady, forced to lean back against the wall.

"What I did? You brought her into this." Artemis turns her attention to me with a smug curl to her lips. "Never forget she deceived you."

Then Artemis disappears in a flash of light.

Ceri removes the crown and kneels as she reaches out to me. Her eyes are restored to their normal cerulean, and the concern I see feels so real that it's easy to forget all that's changed between us now.

I hesitate a moment, but then I take her hand as she helps me stand.

"I'm so sorry. I never expected this to get so out of hand."

Standing makes me dizzy, but she steadies me. I don't miss the strength of her grip, even as she keeps it light to avoid hurting me.

My eyes go to the crown in her other hand. I shake my head. Perhaps it only works if it's on the woman's brow. Even now, I can feel an echo of its power, though, like a distant harp echoing down a long hallway.

"I don't understand how I managed to get that off of Artemis. I was—" I was her fucking, eager bitch. If Ceri put the crown back on and used it on me, I don't think I could resist it again. The sensation of being under its influence was like being constantly on the edge of an orgasm.

"Love." She strokes the left side of my face with her hand, her touch warm and gentle. "The crown isn't more powerful than a true love."

I laugh uneasily. Love. "I've only known you a few days, if that."

"Sometimes, that's all it takes."

She drops the crown to the floor and pulls me to her. My whole body and soul surrenders to her embrace. The kiss isn't quite the same as Ceri's was. Ceri's kisses were less confident but just as passionate.

When we break from the kiss, we nuzzle against one another, my head pressed to her neck and shoulder, breathing in her scent. She still smells like roses.

"And sometimes," she whispers into my ear, "it can take years." She cups my face in her hands as she leans back to look me in the eyes. "The most passionate hearts can belong to many others, and I don't believe Ceri is the only one for you."

"Are you Ceri?" I want her to say she is.

"She's a part of me. If you're willing and patient enough, I'll gladly let you explore more of me."

I stare at her dumbstruck. Aphrodite, the Goddess of Love, is offering to date me. As if my life wasn't strange enough.

"Yes, I want that." My heart aches with the need for her.

"Then I'll be back soon. I promise." Her hands slip away from my face as she steps back and smiles. "Don't neglect the other claims on your heart while I'm gone."

Before I can respond, Ceri and the crown disappear in a flash of light, just as her sister Artemis had.

I consider going into my room to throw on a large t-shirt, but that's too far. I retrieve the half empty bottle of wine from the kitchen counter and collapse onto my sofa, where I quickly drink it before I pass out.

Epilogue: Game Time

It's raining when I knock on Kelly's door the next night.

As soon as she cracks the door open, I raise the bag of cookies.

"If I wasn't so relieved to see you're alive, I'd be pissed about you showing up this late."

"It's only 9:30. That's earlier than the last time."

She shuts the door, undoes the chain, and admits me.

I stroll inside in my black trench coat and hand her the cookies. Kelly doesn't bother asking about coffee this time. She just sets the cookies on the coffee table and starts brewing water.

While she fiddles around in the kitchen, I tell her all that's happened.

"So, let me get this straight," she says as she pours the coffee out of the French press into the mugs. "You have a standing booty call with the Goddess of Love?"

"I think?" I don't bother hiding how uncertain I am of my exact relationship status with Ceri. I still find it difficult to think of her as Aphrodite, and somehow, I think she almost prefers to be Ceri with me. I think about how much she enjoyed me dominating her the other night, and I suspect it was because that almost never happens to a goddess.

Some her powers were still working, because that had to be why all the customers in Avalon were so amorous when I got there and why the truth serum went so sideways.

Kelly hands me my coffee mug as she reclines across from me in her purple fainting chair. "So, dare I ask if you're still getting paid?"

"Funny you should mention that." I wiggle my phone in the air between us, as if there was something on there for her to see. "Checked my bank account this morning, and seems even Greek gods have bank accounts, because I had a hundred thousand dollars deposited in there."

I don't think I've ever seen someone's eyeballs actually get as big as golf balls until that moment. "You must have learned quite a few tricks since college, because you were good, but you weren't that good."

"I'm sure the bonus is just," I clear my throat, "hazard pay." I quickly retreat into my coffee mug.

"So that's what we're calling that these days."

We both laugh at that.

"All right, so out with it," Kelly scowls at me. "Just what is it you want tonight? Surprised you'd even be taking another case this quickly."

"I don't have a new case yet." I eye her over the rim of my mug as I take a sip.

"So what? You're just visiting to chat over cookies and coffee?"

"Yeah."

Kelly's scowl deepens, clearly not believing me. She sips her coffee and then sets the mug onto the coffee table. "So if you're just paying me a visit, you going to take off your coat and actually stay a while?"

"Well, that depends on you." I reach into one of my coat's pockets and pull out a deck of playing cards, setting them on the coffee table between us. "I was thinking we might play some poker."

"Poker? Really?"

I stand and untie the belt to my trench coat. "Strip poker."

I let the coat drop to the floor, revealing the orange silk dress that Artemis had made me wear to seduce Ceri.

"Although, it might be a very short game for me."

Kelly's jaw falls open.

I lean down towards her, resting my hands on her coffee table while giving her plenty to see as the top of the silk dress hangs dangerously low.

"Would you like to call my bluff?"

About the Author

Alena Cerulean lives in Richmond, Virginia. When she isn't writing something, she can often be found (if you know what she looks like), haunting various coffee shops and bars. She's also worked in a call center for a company that shall go unnamed for the past decade.

You can connect with me on:
- https://twitter.com/AlenaCerulean
- https://www.threads.net/@alenacerulean
- https://www.instagram.com/alenacerulean
- https://bsky.app/profile/alenacerulean.bsky.social

Also by Alena Cerulean

She Comes at Night
When a vampire lives for as many centuries as **Anastasia** has, she knows a good thing when she sees her. So when she enters the Green Witch bar, she instantly decides to claim its delectable owner as her own. The closer she gets to enthralling **Kaci**, the more she realizes her new obsession is hiding something dangerous.

Chase has taken down her share of predators, having hunted monsters for most of her adult life. She also knows better than to get involved with a client, but when the Green Witch's gorgeous owner seeks Chase's help to stop the vampire stalking her, Kaci proves irresistible.

All three women harbor dark secrets, and Chase's hunt for Anastasia threatens to expose all of their past sins and destroy them.

She Comes at Night is a 35,000 word erotica novella full of vampires, mind control (both consensual and forced), lesbian sex, and dom/sub relationships.